How does a dragon tell the woman he loves that it was he who had delivered her into the hands of the enemy?

Enslaved as one of Cewrick's feared black dragons, for centuries Taylith had been forced to do the evil sorcerer's bidding. Finally free of the shackles of slavery, Taylith is enlisted by King Biryn as a member of his elite team.

Plagued with visions of an impending war and the return of the black dragon he once was, Taylith must find a way to tell his lifemate, Laura, that he was the creature that had captured her and delivered her into the hands of the enemy.

To keep Laura safe and save her sister from Zohmes' clutches, he must allow the god to change him back into the feared creature he once was.

Shard in the Mirror
Crimson Realm Chronicles Book 6
Copyright © 2019 Taryn Jameson and Gabriella Bradley
ISBN: 978-1-4874-2463-3
Cover art by Angela Waters

Published by eXtasy Books Inc or
Devine Destinies, an imprint of eXtasy Books Inc
Look for us online at:
www.eXtasybooks.com or www.devinedestinies.com

SHARD IN THE MIRROR

CRIMSON REALM CHRONICLES BOOK 6

BY

TARYN JAMESON
AND
GABRIELLA BRADLEY

DEDICATION

Taryn Jameson –

To the woman who sparked my imagination with her tales of political intrigue, gladiators, and the rise and fall of Rome. This one is for you Mom.

Gabriella Bradley –

To my mother who would have loved this series. I hope she has been looking over my shoulder from above and reading it with me as we write.

CHAPTER ONE

Taylith just managed to catch Laura as her legs buckled. He realized that what she had overheard had shocked her to the core. She had not fainted but was unsteady on her feet and trembled from head to toe. He led her to a chair, then turned to get her a goblet of wine, but she groped for his hand. "Don't leave me, Taylith. Please."

Cewrick filled a goblet and handed it to him. "Here, drink some of this to settle your nerves." Taylith held it to her lips and waited while she took a few sips.

She pushed his hand away. "I was with Julia earlier. How and when did this happen? How can she be pregnant with Zohmes' baby? She was very upset when John died, which showed me she had more than friendship feelings for him. And it's obvious, since he got her pregnant. I don't see how any of what you're saying is possible."

Ciara approached her. "Laura, when John died, Icaras and I erased the memory of his death in those that witnessed it. I will return that memory for you and you will understand." Placing her hand on Laura's forehead, she chanted softly.

Laura's eyes widened. "Oh my God! Zohmes possessed John. He was using his body to get information and get closer to the king. Now I understand the change in him."

Ciara nodded. "Brenn and I need to leave to go to Xynnar

1

to investigate Niqine's abduction. Icaras has gone to the compound to bring back Barry, who was also possessed by Zohmes. Both Julia and Niqine were abducted in the same manner as Cylena."

"How could the bastard be in two places at once?" Laura asked, her voice unsteady.

"He can get from one place to another in a nano second. With us out of the way to rescue Hirsuta, he saw a clear path to abduct Niqine and Julia," Cewrick answered.

"How can she be carrying his baby? It was still John's body Julia was involved with."

Astiana set her goblet on the table. "Zohmes' essence entered John, then took over his body, soul, and mind completely. Their DNA would have mixed."

"Julia needs to have an abortion. She can't have this baby. One devil to fight is enough." She clamped her lips together determinedly.

Taylith was horrified. Jewel dragons lived for centuries before the gods would grant a couple the gift of a child, and now there were no children on the Tideless Abyss. The curse had taken the lives of many, and the children that had survived the forced change were now adults. "If abortion means termination, we do not do that on Ierilia. It might be considered if the mother's life is in peril, but it rarely happens."

"She can't have this baby, Taylith. It's a little Satan. A Zohmes miniature."

Astiana interrupted. "The gods and goddesses will decide what is best. First, we must find out exactly what happened, and where Zohmes took them both, so we can form a plan of action."

He was thankful for Astiana's interruption. Laura's tattered emotions were a constant burn within him, the pain of it staggering. The abduction of Julia and the knowledge that the evil being who had nearly killed her had also fathered the child her sister carried had fractured a part of her soul. His body stiff, he raked his fingers through his hair, his own demons rushing through to the surface, threatening to break free. Gods, he needed to find a way to alleviate her torment before his own anguish overpowered him. He took a deep breath and grabbed a glass from the table, filling it with eldalas spirit.

"Here, this will calm you better than the wine." Taylith handed her a small glass filled with the strong liquor.

After he saw that Laura had calmed down and she continued to fire questions at the others, he excused himself and walked toward the balcony doors. "I need to get some air."

He wiped snow off a bench, sat on it, and gazed at the gray sky. The snow kept on falling steadily, transforming the palace gardens into a pristine, white wonderland untouched by the sorrow that had enslaved his soul. The whole situation was such a tangled web. Julia's kidnapping had broken open Laura's wounds of her own abduction. How could he tell her that it was his dragon that had seized her and had placed her in Cewrick's clutches? That it was because of him she had to endure captivity and torture? The realization that Laura was his lifemate had come to him at the king and queen's joining celebration. He knew he had fallen in love with her, and not just a little bit.

Laura had come to terms with her traumatic experience, or so it seemed, but if she knew the truth? Lifemate or not, would it alienate her? Yet, he had to tell her. He could not pursue a relationship with her based on lies. Although it was not really a lie. She had never asked him if he knew which dragon had abducted her and Mark. It was a truth he kept hidden deep inside his heart.

"Taylith, what is troubling you?"

Ciara's voice startled him out of his thoughts. He and his cousin had always been close. They were only weeks apart in age. Their fathers had been twins and were inseparable before the curse. "Ciara, I need to talk to someone about what plagues my heart and soul. Maybe you can advise me what to do."

Ciara drew her cloak around her and sat beside him. "I have seen the turmoil in your eyes, Taylith. You know you can always come to me to unload your problems."

He gazed into those violet eyes of hers. She always looked upon him with love, but how could she now, knowing the black dragon he had become and that he had forgotten her for centuries. Still, she loved him, even when he had abandoned her to the Clyss. "I know, Ciara. You have always been there when I needed you." He smiled wistfully at her. "But this is very personal."

Ciara placed her gloved hand on his. "Whatever it is will be safe with me. You know that. Does it have anything to do with Laura?"

He nodded. "I have fallen in love with her. I believe her to be my lifemate."

"When the time is right, I can speak to Rania for you."

"I am wrestling with all of it. After centuries of mating with only our own kind, why have the gods and goddesses chosen lifemates for us that are not of our own species? First, you and Brenn, a dragon and a lion. Then Laro and Erica, and now my heart belongs to Laura. I feel my soul reaching out to her."

"Do you think she has feelings for you?"

"Yes. Her behavior, small things, expressions in her eyes, on her face—all tell me she feels the same."

"Then what is the problem? Questioning the gods and

goddesses does not help your situation. If they have chosen Laura to be your lifemate, then it is written in the book of knowledge, and so it shall be."

"How do I know for sure?" Of course he knew the truth of it *now*. There was no other explanation. The moment he had plucked Laura from the compound in Cront, her soul had reached out to his, and unknown to them both, a connection had been made. It was the reason he started coming to his senses before Cewrick's power waned and the curse was lifted.

"I told you. I will talk with Rania. But, Taylith, I know something else is troubling you. I can feel it."

His jaw clenched, he closed his eyes and whispered, "I was the one that abducted Laura and Mark and took them to Cewrick."

Ciara linked her arm through his. "Now I understand. And you *do* need to tell Laura. If she is truly your lifemate, she will forgive you. After all, when Cewrick's powers were depleting, and you regained some of your humanity, you remembered, and it was you who saved her and Mark. You need to speak with her soon and tell her the truth."

He rubbed his forehead. "Gods, I know I need to tell her. The longer I keep the truth from her, the more this wound will fester, but I do not think she can handle it at this time. Julia's disappearance has devastated her, and she is very worried for her sister. It was already too much for her to learn Julia is carrying Zohmes' infant. Her mental state is too fragile. I would risk losing her forever."

"Trust the gods and goddesses, Taylith. What will be, will be."

Trust the gods and goddesses… Taylith did, but they had every right to punish him for the misdeeds he had committed in Cewrick's name. He had only just realized why he was so drawn to Laura. Would the gods give him such a gift, only to whisk it away because of the darkness that had resided in his soul for centuries? "Now that the king has given the people from Earth their own realm, Laura is excited at the prospect of beginning fresh, making a life there. They have already begun making plans and are clearing an area to commence building. If Laura decides to live there, I will barely see her."

"Her excitement over their realm has waned due to Julia's abduction. Also, Laura has accepted a commission to work in our science facility. She is an accomplished botanist and scientist and is working hard to study how Earth's seeds will grow and thrive under Ierilian conditions and if she can help to make it all grow faster. Erica is already pressuring her about her coffee. Laura cannot move too far away from Cront. For now, she is still a guest in our home. Stop worrying needlessly about trivial matters and tackle the main problem of your troubled mind, but you must wait for the right time."

A breeze drove the snow onto the balcony. Ciara wrapped her cloak around her shoulders tighter and shivered. "We need to go inside. Icaras and Aldis are back, and we need to discuss Julia and Niqine's rescue."

"Yes." He had not put on his cloak or gloves, and now he rubbed his chilled hands together. "Will you speak to Rania soon?"

"Yes, I promise, but we have more pressing matters we have to deal with right now, and so does Rania. She is overjoyed at the return of her daughter and is by Hirsuta's side. Now come back in before you freeze to death. It was foolish of you to come and sit out here without your cloak."

He followed her inside. He should have fetched his cloak from his room. After the king had offered him a commission in Brenn's troops and a position on his team, Brenn and Ciara had graciously invited Taylith to be their guest until he found other accommodations. He had accepted happily because it meant being close to his cousin and to Laura. Ciara and her parents were all he had now. He still mourned his own parents, who had presumably been killed while they were black dragons. They never returned after the curse had been lifted and they had all regained their humanity. He fully understood the goddess Rania wanting to be with the daughter she had thought was dead. He could only imagine his own joy if he discovered his family to be alive. He pulled up a chair next to Laura and, reaching out, took her hand in his.

Brenn spoke first. "We have the warrior in custody. He does not seem to remember anything except standing guard in front of Niqine's front door."

"And we have Barry as well. Both prisoners are in a cell in the dungeons," Aldis added.

"Have you questioned them?" Biryn demanded to know.

"Briefly," Aldis said. "Like the guard at Xynnar, Barry does not remember anything that happened."

Laura fidgeted with the small empty glass. "From what you told me, Barry was standing right behind Julia. How could he not remember anything?"

"Zohmes occupied his mind and body just long enough to spirit Julia away. Barry's mind was not his own," Ciara explained patiently.

"He'll still be a pompous ass. John was possessed for quite a long time and that's why he acted so differently. I couldn't imagine Barry being possessed for that length of time. Add Zohmes' demeanor to Barry and he'd be worse than a pompous ass. He would turn into a complete dickhead," Erica muttered.

"So how are we going to rescue my sister? Do we even know where she is?" Laura questioned.

7

Taylith placed his arm around her shoulders and hugged her briefly. "Laura, Julia is carrying Zohmes' infant. I am sure he will treat her well."

Biryn agreed. "Yes. The same for Niqine. Only she knows how to get the book of knowledge. She is extremely fragile. Any mistreatment of her could kill her instantly. Zohmes will try different methods to get the information from her."

Laura sipped from her glass. "Did the return of Niqine and her maidens make a difference to the vegetation and crops in the hothouses?"

Dunmore answered. "I can enlighten you, if I may speak?" When Biryn nodded, he continued. "There has been no change at this point. Niqine was not there for very long. Maybe she needs to be there longer and in the presence of the maidens for their magick to be effective."

Biryn nodded. "Yes, I agree. We need to rescue Niqine fast, or our crops in our hothouses will surely perish. Can the plants and vegetables still recuperate, Laura?"

"At this point, yes. But given the decay, a week will see everything destroyed, and the disease will spread to the farms and other hothouses on those farms."

Aldis stood. "Then we must act fast. Ierilia cannot be without fresh vegetables and fruit. We now know the location of several of Zohmes' temples, and Odoxon's castle. I doubt he is keeping them in any of those. It would make it too easy for us to find them. I am sure he has more secret temples located all over Ierilia for his minions and priests to worship him. I suspect he is holding them in a very difficult to find place. But I am more than tired. I suggest we retire for the night and meet again in the morning."

They all agreed and were just saying goodnight when Biryn's communicator sounded. Taylith noticed the expression on the king's face. He seemed almost reluctant to answer it, but he did and put it on speaker.

It was Catrice. "Your Majesty, Hirsuta is awake and requests her husband's presence. Only Cewrick. She is still very tired."

"Very well. He is already on his way."

Taylith took Laura's hand and walked her to one of the guest rooms. She stopped and turned to him. "I don't want to be alone tonight. Will you stay with me?"

CHAPTER TWO

Taylith paced in front of the bedroom window while Laura readied herself for bed. Every feeling she had experienced slashed through him like a knife. The guilt of Julia's abduction, fear of and *for* the infant her sister carried, and the terror of what Zohmes may do to them both. They *should* be afraid of what Zohmes would and could do. *The infant is related to the king.* None of them had given a thought about who exactly the child was to Biryn. *Of course it all makes sense now. If we for some reason cannot rescue Julia, and Zohmes manages to keep the infant, he probably will raise him to rule Ierilia. Except no one knows yet that the queen has conceived. That will thwart the monster's plans when the news becomes public.*

He turned when the door of the bathroom opened. Laura stepped through, her long, blonde hair spilling around her shoulders. It had grown several inches since he had first set eyes on her, and he longed to thread his fingers through those silky strands. The nightdress she wore must have been part of her clothing from Earth. It came to just above her knees. It had a colored animal on the front much like a youngling's drawing. It had long ears, a pink nose and belly, and big feet. It was holding an axe behind its back. *How odd.* On her feet were pink fluffy shoes that had the same strange animal on them. He shook his head, trying to contain a laugh. How could she possibly look so delectable wearing such a thing?

She patted the animal on her nightshirt, while walking to stand before him. "What...it's Happy Bunny...see?" She pointed to the symbols below the picture. "Cute but psycho. Julia gave it to me when we were accepted into the relocation program."

"Psycho?"

She clasped his hands in hers, a hint of pain flashing in her green eyes. "Yes...just like my life right now. Everything has gone crazy and I feel helpless to stop it."

He pulled her into his arms and studied her face. Outwardly, she seemed to be calm, but he could still feel the tumult of emotions that raged within her. "We will find your sister. The gods will not allow him to keep her or the baby."

"Zohmes tortured and almost killed me. I couldn't bear it if he does the same to Julia." She slid her arms around his neck. "I can't stand to think about it anymore." Standing on her tiptoes, she kissed him, tentatively at first, then forcing his lips apart, passionately.

It was a demand he did not have the power to ignore. The feel of her in his arms, the sweet taste of her lips, ignited a fire within him that could not be quenched. From the moment he had seen her at Ciara's betrothal celebration, he had hungered for her. He had known who she was, what he had done to her. All the time fighting his attraction, he kept his distance. He had no wish to hurt her more than he already had. Each time he had seen her, that connection within him grew stronger, weakening his resolve. When Ciara had asked him to stay at Brenn's estate to protect Laura and the others, he had gladly left the Tideless Abyss just to be near her. He dug his fingers into the sleek softness of her hair while claiming her lips. His hands glided down her back to cup the cheeks of her shapely ass. Lifting her from the floor, he carried her to her bed, gently lowering her onto the soft comforter.

She pulled him down beside her, her lips seeking his, her hands trailing down his chest to the waist of his pants. She whispered, "God, Taylith, I need to forget about tonight."

Taylith stilled, his sanity clawing back to the surface through his passion-soaked mind. He wanted nothing more than to lose himself in her arms, but not when pain was the driving force of her need. He kissed her gently on the cheek and took a deep breath to calm his desire, willing his needy cock to behave. "I cannot, Laura. Not like this."

Laura flopped onto her back on the bed. "Why not? Most men would jump at the chance to have sex, especially with no strings attached."

After spending time with both Laura and Erica, he understood several of their Earth terms, sex was one of them, and he refused to mate with her just for the sake of it. He gazed down at her beautiful face and reached out to caress her cheek. "Because I will not be a tool to help you forget everything that has happened and to ease your pain." He teased her bottom lip with his fingertip and fought the urge to nip it with his teeth. "Because I want more than you are ready to give."

"Like what?" she murmured while tugging at the string at the top of his pants.

He gently took her hand and placed it on his chest. "Laura, we have become very close."

She toyed with the laces of his tunic, pulling several free. "Yes. Besides Julia, you are my best friend. Almost like the big brother I never had."

Best friend? Brother? He groaned inwardly. "What if I want to be more than a friend or brother? And do brothers and sisters mate on Earth?"

She giggled. "No, brothers and sisters do not mate. That's just disgusting." She maneuvered her fingers beneath the material of his tunic to caress his chest. "But *friends* sometimes do. It's called friends with benefits."

He tenderly stroked her face, then, playing with her hair, looked down into her eyes. "My sweet, I understand your need, but what drives it is your troubled mind and soul. What you want will give you a brief respite only. Like I said before, I desire more than that. You are more precious to me than you realize."

"I value our friendship, Taylith." She uttered a long sigh. "Just stay with me, then? Hold me?"

There was that word again. *Friendship*. After she relaxed on the pillows, he lay beside her and took her into his arms. Stroking her hair, he watched her eyelids finally droop. Tenderly cradling her, he wished she returned his feelings. But it was too soon. In a way he felt relieved. He wanted her heart, her soul, her love, but if and when the time came for her to reciprocate his desires, he would have to tell her the truth. For now, he would have to be satisfied with friendship and camaraderie. Still pondering on his dilemma, he drifted off into a restless slumber.

Clouds surrounded Taylith as if he were in flight between realms to the Tideless Abyss. The great, billowy white masses shifted like a cyclone, parting to expose a very large crystal book. Etchings covered it in a language he couldn't read. He had never seen such a tablet before, but deep down he knew it had to be the book of knowledge. Stories had been told, fables passed down through generations from those that were created first. A fierce wind curled around him, whipping his hair around his face. The tempest ripped the book open. Pages rapidly turned, then abruptly stopped. A bright light flashed, almost blinding him. He covered his eyes to shield them, then carefully peeked through his fingers. A thin streak of fire blazed, scrawling across the pages, imprinting the words that had and would proclaim destiny – past, present, and future. Suddenly the pages flipped backward, words changed, were being re-written, shifting forward again. The strange inscriptions continued, then changed. Symbols no longer flowed from the blade of fire. A vision materialized before him. A dream he was very much a part of.

A giant man, black as ink, silver hair hanging in a braid down his shoulder, shouted a battle cry. An army dressed in black armor, their faces hidden beneath spiked helmets, surged forward from a coiling dark abyss. In their hands were long, pointed spikes. Eerie green tendrils of magick snaked around them, shielding them from harm. The wind picked up speed and more pages turned. A massive swirling sphere of fire, followed by a trail of flames, traveled at blasting velocity through a dark sky, hurtling toward a shadowed planet. And still the pages kept turning and the quill of fire continued to write and draw.

Two men engaged in a raging battle, the sound of swords clashing reverberating around them. Brothers at war, a house divided. A grotesque face painted the sky above spiking mountain peaks. A black temple stood in the distance, surrounded by a haze of fog. Robed priests performed a ritual upon an altar the color of blood. A large ornate wooden door stood behind it, a green light glowing eerily through the keyhole.

A long cylinder of fire, blazing like the suns, illuminated an obsidian sky. The beat of wings, a dragon swarm, the dragons with black-as-pitch scales flying stealthily in the night. A great, scarred beast flew with them. Somehow he realized the beast was Zohmes' pet. Below, foul creatures drank from a lake of blood, the scent of death permeating the air. The shadowed figure of a man stood beside the lake. Magick issued from his fingertips. Taylith saw an ornate key of gold with swirling designs wrapped around the base all the way to the top. A winged creature formed the head of the key and a living red dragon's eye glowed and moved in the center of its body.

The eye looked directly at him, drawing him to it. The team needed it. He knew it. He reached out to grab it, but it disintegrated into dust, the fragments slowly coming together again, once again forming a large key as it continued falling into the bloody water below.

A figure emerged from the bloody liquid, covered in red. It appeared to be a woman, triumphantly holding up the key in one hand, in the other, half of a soul shard.

More pages turned, then stopped. The shaft of fire continued to scrawl, pictures floating before his eyes so close, he could almost touch them. A spaceship darkened the light of the suns. Explosions hurled chunks of debris. Screams rent the air. Frightened mobs of people ran to avoid the onslaught of fire and falling refuse, many becoming victims of the inferno that raged around them.

The book snapped shut, and the fiery scribe disappeared. A booming voice echoed around him. "I am the maker of all gods and goddesses, of magick, and the creator of all that is, was, and shall be. It is as it was written, and so it shall be done, and be forever more. I have spoken."

Taylith woke with a start, his body trembling, his heart pounding in his sweat-lathered chest. He sat up, disoriented, while his mind cleared of the horrible visions and his eyes focused on his surroundings. The palace. He was in a guest room. *Laura's room.* Yet the clouds, the wind, and the book — the visions — had seemed so real. He could still hear the deep timber of that voice in his ears, feel the heat of fire on his skin. The stench of death still hung heavily in the air. He knew what had been shown to him was no dream. Was it the past? The present? Or was it a very possible future that was now inscribed firmly into the book of knowledge? The god had told him, it is as it was written, and so it shall be done. The black dragons, the priests, the lake of blood — the key. Memories of his slavery to Cewrick burst free of the cage they were trapped in. He knew of the lake. He had heard talk of it from Cewrick's minions, and there was only one way to get to it. *The great scarred beast.* He was going to be sick. That scarred beast was him, his black dragon. What the gods required of him was a steep price to pay for their forgiveness. And how was he going to explain to the team what he had seen? Maybe he was reading too much into it.

He had lost track of how the pages had turned. Could a portion of the vision have been of the past? Much of the past had been lost to him. He had regained some of his memories, but not all. A gift from the gods, he supposed. If the gods had allowed him full memory of his time as a black dragon, he doubted he could bear the truth of what he had been and what he had done. He took a slow, deep breath to calm his nausea. Then, rubbing his face with his hands, he realized the bed was empty. He had been so deeply ensnared by the visions, he had not noticed Laura had left. *Thank the gods for that.* She had her own monsters to battle, and there was no way he could hide the demons that rode him at that moment.

He tried to clear his mind by picturing Laura. She had slept so quietly in his arms most of the night, but he worried what state her mind was in this morning. The horror of the visions and his own emotions hammering away at him overshadowed anything he might have felt from their connection.

Still shaken from the visions he had been granted, he bathed and dressed quickly, then headed to the king's quarters. He was so absorbed in his thoughts he practically knocked Ciara off her feet when he bumped into her. She and Brenn arrived at Biryn's door the same time he did.

Ciara cast him a troubled glance, then looked at Brenn. "Give us a moment?"

After Brenn had entered Biryn's chambers, she clasped

Taylith's hands, tendrils of her magick spreading through him, helping to calm him.

"Taylith, what is it?"

Gods, he knew he had to tell her and the team what he had been shown, but for now, he would omit the scarred black dragon. He would deal with that if and when the time came. "The gods have given me a vision."

CHAPTER THREE

Everyone else was already in Biryn's dining room and sitting around the table, eating breakfast. Taylith was grateful to see the empty chair next to Laura. "Morning, sweet lady," he told her softly so only she would hear.

Ciara's magick had helped temper most of his unease, but he still did not have an appetite. Laura looked at him questioningly and began to heap food on his plate, when Biryn tapped on the table with his fork. He sighed in relief. He was not ready to answer her questions at the moment.

"Cewrick has something to tell us. Cewrick?"

Cewrick stood. "I spent the night sitting beside Hirsuta. She is doing well and recovering. During the night, the goddess Rania appeared to us and told us where Zohmes is keeping Julia and Niqine. He has a temple in the Sirona realm. There is a mountain ridge called Dreaded Peaks. It is not too far from Wildevein and Lord Milhella's estate. It is called so because anyone that has ever ventured into the ridge has never returned. There have been sightings of monsters. Clouds always surround the peaks."

"Sirona is quite a distance from here," Aldis stated.

"The goddess also warned that Lord Milhella is in league with Zohmes and Odoxon."

"Cidus?" Biryn frowned. "I have known him many years. He and his son, Evior, attended our joining celebration."

Cewrick nodded. "The son rebels against the father. Rania said he may be of help to us. I would like to remain here with Hirsuta, but the goddess told me I must go with you."

Laura interrupted. "I want to go, too. She is my sister."

Taylith patted her arm. "It is far too dangerous, Laura."

She raised her chin, a determined look in her eyes. "I don't care. I need to go along. I can fight just as well as the rest of you."

Biryn disagreed. "Taylith is right. You have no idea the dangers we face on these missions."

She stiffened her shoulders. "I don't care. Julia practically raised me after our parents died and was there for me when... I need to go. I can't just sit here and wait and worry. It will drive me crazy."

"Biryn, if you will allow her to go with us, I will watch over her." Taylith squeezed Laura's hand. He did not like the idea of her going on the mission, but Laura was headstrong and stubborn. They had clashed several times during his duty to guard her and Brenn's guests. If she was not allowed to go, he knew she would find a way to set out on her own to try to save her sister. He wondered what she had been going to say when she had stopped mid-sentence.

"Very well. But she is your responsibility. The only one exempt from this mission is the queen."

Taylith nodded gratefully. "Thank you. I will contact some more of my dragon friends eager to serve the king and queen, to guard Cylena."

"Good. Aldis, what have you discovered about our destination?"

Aldis had his datapad open and brought up a holograph of the region. "It is very dangerous terrain. We will use a hovercraft but will not be able to land it within the ridge. That means climbing and hiking, unless Icaras, Ciara, and Astiana can magically transport us. Cewrick, did Rania give any indication where the temple is located?"

"No. She only said that Cidus' son might be able to assist us. Maybe he knows where it is?"

Taylith took the last bite of his breakfast. "Do we really want strangers involved in our missions?"

"Rania told us the son can help. We must at all times listen to the goddess, Taylith. Isn't there something you need to tell us?" Ciara asked impatiently.

Ciara reminding him of his vision caused instant perspiration to dot his forehead. Taylith wiped his brow with his napkin. Murmurs around the table had stopped, and he saw their expectant faces blur for a moment. Pulling himself together, he began. "Early this morning I was granted a vision. It was not like anything I have ever experienced. It was so real, so vivid, that I still shudder at the memory of it."

"Who gave you the vision, Taylith?" Ciara asked.

"He gave no name and told me he was the maker of all gods and goddesses, of magick, and the creator of all that is, was, and shall be."

"I do not know of anyone besides the gods and goddesses of ever receiving such a gift," Ciara exclaimed.

Taylith frowned at the interruption. He just wanted to get it over with. "Why he chose me is a mystery. I saw a shaft of fire writing in what I think is the book of knowledge. We have to go to a lake. Its water is like blood. The stench of death surrounds it. I saw monstrous creatures drinking from its waters. In it lies a key. A woman surfaced from the water, holding it. We must obtain that key to gain entrance to the temple. I saw a bloody altar surrounded by Zohmes' priests. Two identical men that were fighting. A fiery ball hurtling toward a planet. A spaceship raining fire upon us, people running and hiding in fear. A giant black man with a silver braid and his army of warriors. It was all such a crazy jumble, I did not know if it was past, present, or future. The only present time I can decipher is the lake of blood, the key, and the altar."

Ciara pushed her tablet toward him. "Taylith, would it be easier for you to record it all?"

He took the tablet, relieved that he would not have to repeat the visions again. "Yes. I think so."

Ciara took a sip from her milk. "I know of this place. It is cursed and is called Blood Lagoon. The red water comes from minerals on the bottom of the lake, causing it to be red and appear like blood. The minerals are highly toxic. Only monsters and creatures would be able to drink from it because it gives them added strength. If a human or normal animal drank its toxic waters, they would die a terrible death. No one can enter the lake. Deformed trees and shrubbery surround it, and it is located in the center of a crater on top of a mountain."

"How do you know of it, Ciara?" Icaras questioned.

"My dragon flew over it centuries ago before I was cursed. I had forgotten its existence."

"Where is it? If a human cannot enter its waters, who is the woman surfacing with the key?" Cewrick asked.

Ciara shrugged. "It is located between the realms of Sirona and Ugaron. As for the woman, I do not know. Maybe this being will speak to Taylith again and give more clarification."

"Wait a minute. I thought Izarus told us he was the god of all gods and goddesses?" Biryn reminded them.

Ciara pulled a face. "I also thought that Izarus was the highest of them all. So maybe he is the god all the gods and goddesses answer to? This entity that spoke to Taylith has never spoken to anyone that I know of. We also have never known who created the book of knowledge and writes in it."

Taylith had moved to a corner of the room and busied himself recording his vision onto the datapad. The visions were still etched into his brain as clear as when the gods had shown them to him.

Laura joined him. His heart warmed as she placed her hand on his knee. "Can I help at all?"

He smiled at her. "Sweet lady, no. I am the only one that can record what I saw and heard."

"I'm so glad you spoke up for me. Don't worry. I can hold my own with a sword. When we trained, we had to learn all manner of defense. That included fencing."

"Fencing?"

"A manner of sword fighting."

"We will have our fleet weapons with us, too, Laura."

"Ah, good. I'm a sharpshooter. Did you know that?"

"What does that mean?"

"It means I can outshoot almost anyone from a great distance."

"There is so much of you I still need to learn. This mission will be dangerous. The unknown god showed me."

"Julia is my older sister. You have no idea what she went through to take care of me after our parents died. I will do anything for her."

"You heard my vision. Does it not scare you?"

"Scare me? No. It sounds kind of exciting. Adventurous."

Taylith sighed. "I know I promised the king that I will take care of you, but I am still not sure you should go with us."

"Taylith, do you know what a gut feeling is?"

He shrugged. "No. More Earth language that does not translate well."

"Have you ever felt deep down within your body that you need to do something? That you have to do it?"

"Yes. Like my *gut*, as you call it, is telling me you should stay behind."

"The king has agreed to let me go along. I refuse to stay here and do nothing. I've made up my mind because my gut tells me I am needed. You can't talk me out of it."

"You are a stubborn woman. Now let me finish putting the complete vision into this datapad for Ciara."

Her head nestled on his shoulder and she stopped talking. Taylith wanted so much to just throw the datapad away, pick her up, and carry her far away to safety. When would she be ready to accept him as her lifemate? His soul yearned for her. His heart already belonged to her. His body ached every moment of the day to make her his. *I love you.* Those three little words just begged to be uttered aloud.

After a while, he finally closed the datapad and looked down at her head resting on his shoulder. She was sound asleep. He smiled. He would let her rest a little while.

Ivran interrupted their peaceful interlude. "Taylith, Laura, we are waiting for you."

Taylith had drifted off himself. Ivran's interruption startled him rudely. "Sorry. Yes, I am finished. We'll come back right away."

Laura jumped up. "Did I fall asleep? Oh my God. Sorry."

They followed Ivran back to the table. He said with a mischievous grin, looking back at them, "Maybe you two were a little busy last night?"

Taylith punched him in the back. "Hush. What does Erica call you?" He glanced at Erica. She had obviously heard, because she grinned from ear to ear.

"Is Ivran being a pain in the ass again?" Erica giggled.

Taylith pulled Laura's chair out for her to sit, then handed the datapad to Ciara. "That's approximately how I saw and heard it all."

"Thank you." Ciara took the datapad and stood. "I am going to seek some privacy for a little while. I will be back soon."

Ciara had already scanned what Taylith had recorded. In the privacy of Biryn's bedroom, she called on the goddess. "Rania, I need you. Please come?"

Rania appeared. "Ciara, what can I do for you? It must be urgent to call me from my daughter's side."

"I thought Izarus was the creator and god of all gods and goddesses."

"No. There is one that created everything. He without a name. Very few in history have ever heard his voice. When queried, his answer has always been I Am who I Am, have been, and shall be forever more."

"Why have you never told me about this deity?"

"Child, would it have mattered? He, who is I Am, leaves all decisions to Izarus and the gods and goddesses."

"He has spoken to Taylith and has given him visions of the book of knowledge."

"Then I Am has favored Taylith for some unknown reason. The one that created everything that ever has been and shall be, rules over us all. Listen to what I Am has told and shown Taylith. I Am decrees our roles in life, our future, the destiny and path of the whole universe and beyond."

"Can you help us decipher the visions?"

"Child, Taylith already has most of the answers you seek. He just needs to accept what he was shown."

"Thank you, Rania."

"I will return to be by my daughter's side. I wish you all the gods and goddesses' strength on the task ahead of you."

"I have some answers," Ciara announced as she sat down.

Taylith frowned. "After reading what I recorded?"

"Yes."

Biryn spoke. "Time is slipping by fast. We need to start on this mission. I advise everyone to get ready. Laura, you will find suitable clothing in your room. I have ordered the kitchen staff to ready packs for us. They will be delivered to my quarters shortly. I suggest we leave after lunch. Now what are the answers?"

"The super deity has been hidden from us for many years. Taylith is privileged that he has been granted a vision and the deity has spoken with him. Before Izarus, there was a deity called I Am. He created what is and has designed whatever was, is, and will be. No one knows who or what this deity is."

"Can we trust it?" Brenn wondered.

"Rania knows of the deity. Yes, we can trust it. It created all of us."

Biryn interjected. "It is almost like we are pawns. Someone is playing with us like we are icons on a battle game board."

"Speak with caution. Whatever we say can be heard," Ciara answered.

Laura spoke up. "I suddenly see a game in my mind. People used to play it on Earth. Some god controlled all the characters and made them kill each other."

Taylith squeezed her hand. "So you think this deity is controlling us all?"

Laura sighed. "I don't know. It seems awfully familiar."

"But Earth people do not believe in the gods and goddesses like we do. Neither do they have the ability to see, hear, and speak with them like us."

"Yes. You're right, though it is written in Earth history that centuries ago there were cultures that believed in many gods and goddesses, much like Ierilia. But history doesn't tell us that they could speak with them and hear them."

"Except in the Bible," Erica said. "God spoke to Moses, and many saw and spoke with angels. But in modern times it is unheard of."

"We will leave after lunch. Be ready." Biryn slammed his fist on the table.

Taylith held his hand out to Laura. They had been dismissed by the king. "We have several hours before lunch, and I need to ensure the queen has her guards in place before we leave. Would you like to fly with me?"

She screwed her face up. "I would like nothing better, but I have to go to the lab and assign someone to oversee my research while I am away. Erica would strangle me if something happened to those coffee plants."

His breath caught when Laura pulled his head down and planted a kiss on his lips. With the kiss still lingering, he headed to the courtyard and shifted into his dragon. All he could think about as he flew through the skies to the Tideless Abyss was the woman who was meant to be his lifemate. The visions of the night before had been pushed to the farthest reaches of his mind.

CHAPTER FOUR

After a quick lunch, they left the king's chambers for the courtyard where the hovercraft awaited them. Taylith wondered if Brenn and Aldis had enough time to figure out where they were going. To the lake of blood, yes. Were Ciara's directions accurate? Questions kept plaguing his mind. From what he knew of Blood Lagoon after he had researched it, it was like Garissa Island—partially of the Ierilian realms but also in the realm of the gods. It could not be accessed by hovercraft or flyers. Even the gods themselves could not transport them to the putrid lake. Zohmes had confiscated it as a place to house his creatures. The only way to get to the island was as one of his pets. A vision of the black beast flashed in his mind. He had withheld a vital piece of information in his recounting of the visions. He knew the change would have to happen, but when? How in the gods' names was he going to change back to a black dragon? And who were the other black dragons?

Laura bumped her shoulder into his arm, drawing his attention. "We are loading up." She grabbed his wrist when he reached down to pick up his pack. "Are you okay, Taylith? You have been so quiet."

He nodded. "I'm still trying to decipher the visions."

They boarded the hovercraft. Taylith took the seat beside Laura and strapped himself in. Astiana, who sat on the other side of him, gave him a troubled glance. Just what he needed was to be seated by the goddess. He knew the gods and goddesses were gifted with the power to read a person's thoughts. Did she know his?

"Our coordinates are the ridge of mountains between Sirona and Ugaron. We will land at the base of the mountains and make camp there." Aldis punched the coordinates into the flight console.

"Ciara said she flew over it before Cewrick's curse. That was centuries ago. How do we know this Blood Lagoon is still there?" Erica queried.

"We don't, other than what the vision has shown Taylith. But it is a starting point," Brenn stated.

Taylith winced as a sharp pain pierced his skull. Visions pierced his mind. *The scarred dragon, the shape rising from the lagoon, covered in red. The figure was suddenly encompassed by a bright flare of light. When the light faded, Laura stood holding the key and half a soul shard. A woman lay upon a bed in a palatial room, an urn of gold stood upon an altar illuminated by a bright glow. A large black bird soaring in the clouds. It held a chain and pendant from its sharp curving beak.* Then as quickly as it had appeared, the vision vanished.

He closed his eyes and leaned his head back against the seat until the pain ceased, praying to the gods that what he had just seen was wrong. But the sick feeling of dread in the pit of his stomach told him that what he had been shown was written in stone. It also explained Laura's stubborn insistence to go with them.

He opened his eyes when a hand touched his arm. Astiana's soft voice flowed through his mind. *Child, seek me after we make camp. I understand your fear, but you have secrets that need to be told, and I am the only one that can help you.* Had she seen and shared the vision he had just been given?

The rest of the flight to Sirona had gone quietly. Aldis landed the craft at the base of Dreaded Peaks in a clearing at the edge of the Wildevein Forest. The forest encompassed much of the area along the mountain range and many miles inward until it reached the outskirts of Lord Cidus' estate. On the other side of the mountain range lay the realm of Ugaron.

After they had set up camp, Taylith gazed at the craggy spines of the mountain. Hidden within the highest peak had to be the temple he was shown, he could feel it. Blood Lagoon, the crater that housed it and the sharp spikes of rock surrounding it, were nowhere to be seen, just as he had suspected. The vision he had been given in the hovercraft flashed through his mind. He turned away from the foreboding mountain range and sought Astiana. If there was any way the goddess could help, he would take it. Somehow, he had to keep Laura safe.

He found Astiana sitting upon a large rock near the outer rim of their campsite. She looked almost peaceful except for the pained expression in her eyes when she gazed up at him.

She motioned for him to join her. "You are no longer the black dragon enslaved to Zohmes, Taylith. Your lifemate will forgive you."

He sank down on the rock to sit beside her. Of course Astiana would know Laura was his lifemate. "But how can you be so sure? I delivered her to Cewrick. She almost died at his hands."

She patted his arm. "Just as she has seen the truth of Cewrick's soul, she knows the truth of yours. Now, child, tell me what you have kept hidden from us."

He raked his fingers through his hair and told her of the scarred beast and the vision he had seen in the hovercraft. "I still haven't made sense of it all myself. I understand the black dragon and why the need for me to change, but why would Laura be the figure emerging from the lake? No human can enter it. And why would she hold half of a soul shard?"

She patted his arm. "To save Julia and Niqine we must have the key, and only the one who has the most to lose can enter the Blood Lagoon. Laura's soul is tied to her sister, the infant, and you. If she does not retrieve the key, many souls will be lost, including her own, and Ierilia will fall to Zohmes."

"Then tell me what I need to do to keep Laura and her sister safe?"

She gave him a penetrating stare. "You must give me your soul shard. For Laura to enter the lagoon, she must wear your shard to protect her soul...and yours. But Zohmes must also be in possession of your shard for us to enter the realm of the Blood Lagoon."

His heart sank. Once Zohmes had possession of even a small part of his soul, he would not be able to become human again. Zohmes would change him and he would be enslaved again, but this time he would have full knowledge of who and what he was. Could Zohmes bend him to his will? It was a dangerous game they played, and he was helpless to stop it.

He handed the goddess his soul shard and watched as she clasped it in her hand. A soft glow emanated around her as the goddess chanted her spell. When her chanting ceased, the glow dissipated, and she opened her hand. In her palm lay two pendants. Each pendant held half of his soul shard ornately wrapped by gold filigree attached to a golden chain.

She gave him the pendants and, grasping his hand in hers, she held his gaze. "You must tell Laura the truth of who you are—of what you are to each other, before Zohmes steals your shard. Tell her when you give her the pendant."

Astiana stood and left him to his thoughts. He gazed at the pendants in his hand. They looked like any other bauble you could purchase at the markets, but what lay inside the intricate weave of gold was a promise, a gift each dragon shared with their potential lifemate before they truly joined at the Clyss. He took one of the pendants and placed it around his neck, the other he stuck in his pocket, then went in search of Laura.

Taylith found her examining the plant life growing around her tent. Even though the ground was covered in snow, bushes of evergreens and berries pushed through the white blanket, providing sustenance for the korobeast and other small animals that made their home in the forest. She turned and smiled at him as he approached.

Taylith clasped her hands in his and leaned down, gently kissing her lips.

Laura gasped in surprise, then gave him a searching look. "Are you okay? Is it the visions?"

He brushed her hair from her face. "I am fine, sweetness, but I have to tell you something important. I need you to listen, not with your mind, but with your heart and soul."

She placed her arms around his neck and hugged him. He closed his eyes and savored the feel of her in his embrace. "We are friends, Taylith. You can talk to me about anything. That is what friends do. They are there for each other."

Friends. He was beginning to hate that word. But after she heard who he was, he may not even have a friendship with her. He gently disengaged her arms and stepped out of her hold, then reached in his pocket and pulled out his soul shard. He placed it around her neck. She was about to speak when he placed his finger across her lips. "No questions. Let me finish."

She nodded her assent.

"First, I need for you to wear this pendant at all times. Do not take it off for any reason. It will protect you." He tucked the pendant beneath the neck of her top, hiding it from view, then played with a strand of her honey-blonde hair. *The crystal is called a soul shard. Dragons gift a piece of their souls to their potential lifemates before their joining ceremony, and it is held within the crystal.*

"How is it that I can hear you? But wh—"

He leaned down and kissed her tenderly. "Because you are my lifemate and you are wearing my shard, and our mission is perilous. I will keep you safe, even if I cannot be there physically."

He felt her confusion riding along their connection and stopped her before she could speak again. "I know you have questions, but I have more to tell you. Let me…please?"

She gestured with her hands for him to continue, then crossed her arms over her chest and tapped her foot on the ground impatiently.

His stomach churned. He closed his eyes. *Just tell her and be done with it.* "I was the black dragon that captured you and Mark."

He heard her suck in a deep breath. Then she slugged him in the jaw. Her words came out in a rush as she pummeled his chest with her fists. "You *asshole*! You knew all this time and you *hid* the truth from me? You could have told me!"

He grabbed her hands to stop her assault and gazed down at her. Tears rolled down her cheeks and anger radiated from her. He expected nothing less, but at least she had not stormed off. "Gods, I am so sorry…I was under the curse."

She pulled a hand away and punched him hard in the chest. "I'm not stupid. I know it was Zohmes. Just as he controlled Cewrick, he owned and controlled all the black dragons." She wiped the tears from her face, pain contorting her features. "You are the one person I trusted not to keep secrets from me... So why are you telling me now? You could have picked a better time, like when we weren't stuck together on this damn mission. Oh wait...or how about when we first met? Before I actually started to like you?"

He tried to pull her into his arms, but she pushed his hands away. A sigh escaped his lips. Her anger he could deal with. At least it was not hatred. "The only way to get to Blood Lagoon is to allow Zohmes to change me back into that creature. For that he needs my soul shard." He held up the pendant that hung around his neck. *Astiana split the shard in two.*

"What in the hell, Taylith? You knew that, too? Before we left?" She growled at him and grabbed him by the arm, then tried to drag him to the fire where the others were roasting meat and talking. He allowed it.

"Uh oh, looks like we have a bit of a lovers' quarrel." Ivran pulled his meat from the fire.

"Ivran, this is not the time to tease," Astiana chastised him.

Laura stopped in front of the group and pushed him forward. "Tell them, Taylith."

Gods, he felt like an antuar caught in a trap, but he could not keep the information from the team any longer. The clock was ticking, and the change would be upon him.

Ciara gave him a concerned look. "Tell us what?"

He studied each of his team members. The gods had exacted a price from them all. He would be no different. He sat beside Laura at the fire. She punched him in the arm and mouthed "tell them" to him.

"Blood Lagoon is no longer located in this realm. It is like Garissa Island and is owned by Zohmes." He filled in the gaps of the vision he had been given and relayed what he had seen on the trip to Sirona, though he left out that Astiana had split his soul shard. Only Ciara and Astiana would know Laura wore it around her neck. It was a secret the dragons held tightly. To own a soul shard was to own the dragon, as Cewrick's evil had shown. There were too many ears within the forest to speak of it out loud.

Ciara's voice sounded in his mind. *Laura wears your soul shard.*

He brushed his hair out of his face and answered. *Only half. Zohmes must steal the other for us to find the Blood Lagoon.*

Ciara held his gaze, her violet eyes filled with pain. *We will find another way to get to the realm. I cannot bear to lose you again.*

He shook his head and smiled wistfully at her. *It is the gods' will and it has been written. There is no other way.*

The bushes rustled, and a man stepped out of the trees to approach the fire.

"Evior, what brings you out to the forest so late?" Biryn asked the newcomer.

Evior bowed to the king, then joined them on the ground in front of the fire. "I am on a hunting expedition and camped not far from here. I saw the glow of your campfire and decided to investigate."

"It is good that you found our encampment. Here, join us for dinner." Aldis handed Evior a stick of meat.

"What can you tell us about the Dreaded Peaks? There is not much in our databases, so I have decided to form my own expedition to visit them myself," Biryn commented.

Evior grimaced. "Why would anyone want to climb the Dreaded Peaks? They were named so for a reason. Fearsome monsters and deadly creatures live on the other side. It is also the home of a temple."

"A temple?" Erica asked, feigning surprise. "Do you know where it is? Sounds intriguing."

"Yes, tell us about it?" Laro added a new piece of meat to

his stick.

"Have you heard of the evil god Zohmes and his sorcerer friend Odoxon?" When they all nodded, he continued. "It is their temple. My father visits it regularly."

"Lord Cidus is able to pass by the monsters?" Taylith looked at the young man. He seemed honest, but could this be a trap?

"Yes. Father insisted I accompany him once. I had no idea what was behind that iron door."

Biryn leaned forward. "What did you see?"

"I saw no monsters or creatures. Father told me they only appear if strangers approach the temple. The door is not an ordinary door. It appears to be solid metal and engraved with strange markings and skulls. There is a large keyhole in its center. But Father needed no key. The sheet of metal magically slid up into the rock facing, allowing us to enter."

"Then what happened?" Cewrick questioned.

"There were a lot of cloaked men and women, all wearing a cowl, so I could not see their faces. The cavern is craggy with red slime dripping down its walls. It resembles blood. At the back of the cavern is a stone altar. It also has strange symbols etched into it. On top stood several candelabras of pure gold with black burning candles. In the center was a large urn. Ten priests surrounded the altar, all wearing red, hooded cloaks. I could not see them very well. Each priest held a gold staff topped by a gold skull. The skulls' sockets had red stones in them and they glowed. They began to chant. The worshippers echoed that chant. It was some kind of gathering that I found out my father attends every week. He wanted me to be initiated, but I refused. I cannot begin to tell you what else I witnessed."

Biryn stood and approached Evior, placing his hand on the young man's shoulder. "Tell us everything. Do not be afraid."

Taylith shuddered and wondered what he would hear next.

Evior looked pleadingly at the king. "Do I have to?"

"Yes, you do. The king needs to know everything that happens on Ierilia," Astiana told him.

"They sacrificed a young woman," Evior muttered softly. "The memory of it gives me nightmares."

Ciara spoke reassuringly. "After you tell us, I can erase that memory for you."

"You can? Thank you, but no thank you. I hate my father for belonging to that cult. If I have no memory of it, then everything will seem normal. Father hates me as much for not agreeing to join."

"Then I will help erase at least the nightmares and ease your troubled mind, after which you can sleep peacefully," Ciara told him.

"They tortured that poor girl. She did not die until they removed her heart. Then they cut her up into pieces, and like cannibals, all the worshippers ate her flesh. The priests shared the heart. Zohmes and Odoxon appeared suddenly and they consumed her eyes. When I refused what they handed me, I thought they would kill me, too. I would not repeat the vows they wanted me to say, so the sorcerer placed a spell on me. I can never again cross the Dreaded Peaks."

Taylith felt sick to the stomach. Julia and Niqine were held in such a monstrous environment? He watched Ciara join Evior and place her hand on his forehead. She chanted softly.

"Thank you, milady," Evior whispered. "I feel so much better. I must go. My men will wonder where I am. Thank you all for sharing your meal with me. May the gods and goddesses protect you."

CHAPTER FIVE

"**H**e spoke truthfully," Ciara told them all after Evior had left them.

"Why does he not leave his father? If my father was involved with Zohmes and Odoxon, I would not live with him," Taylith stated.

"I am very surprised with what he told us. Cidus? He has always been a royal supporter." Biryn threw his stick in the fire.

"I am surprised he attended the celebration," Ciara said.

Erica snorted. "Maybe he meant to cause trouble and didn't succeed? Or he has two faces, one that sucks up to the king, and the other in league with the two bastards."

Crackling of twigs and the rustling of shrubbery caused them to look toward the sound. Taylith thought maybe Evior had returned. He, Brenn, Ivran, Erica, and Laro all stood ready, holding their swords. A bent figure appeared. It was an old woman. Her straggly gray hair hung in greasy strings to her waist. A gnarled hand held a misshapen stick. She was dressed in what could only be called rags. Her face looked centuries old, it was so creased and parchment-like.

Taylith watched her approach him. For some reason he knew this creature was not the old bent woman she appeared to be, that the time had come for Zohmes to steal his soul shard. He lowered his sword as the woman stopped directly in front of him, then asked in a croaky voice, "I am so hungry. Do you have a coin for me, so I can buy food?"

Playing along with the creature's game, he twisted sideways to dig a coin out of his pocket. The woman suddenly snatched the chain around his neck and yanked. It fell to the ground. Instantly, at the gasps of the team, the woman shifted into a large, fearsome bird. The stick she had carried fell to the ground and became a hissing snake. Erica jumped forward and cut its head off. The bird soared upward, holding the chain and his soul shard in its curved beak.

Aldis aimed and fired at it, but it was too late. Taylith saw the bird disappear behind the ridge into the cloud bed that surrounded the peaks.

Snow began to fall again. Taylith gazed up at the sky, still stunned from what had just happened. He rubbed his neck where the skin had chafed as the old woman had ripped the chain off. "And now it begins," he mumbled.

Laura stood beside him. She appeared calmer. "Now it begins? What does that mean?"

Astiana gestured at the group to sit. "It means we do not have much time to plan. The change will be upon Taylith soon."

Taylith walked along the edge of the camp. It hadn't taken long for the team to formulate a plan, but what good could it possibly do? They were at the whim of the gods, and I Am had not shown him the others at the lake of blood. There was only Laura, the beast, and an unknown sorcerer.

The sound of footsteps crunched on the icy blanket of snow. Laura walked up beside him, huddled in a blanket. "I spoke to Ciara and Erica. They explained to me exactly what a lifemate means." She pulled the pendant from under her shirt and held it in her hand. "Ciara told me what *this* means. I asked them because I wasn't sure you would be honest with me. She also told me your vision and which part I must play in my sister's rescue."

Gods, he could still feel how angry she was. It was raw and sore like a festering wound. "I am sorry I didn't tell you, but would you have believed me then? Would you have forgiven the actions I had no control over?"

He took the shard from her hand and, after slipping the chain over her head, tucked it back under her top. *Please, keep it hidden. The forest has ears, and without my soul shard, you will not be safe. You must have it to survive the Blood Lagoon.*

Her eyes widened in surprise, a confused expression on her face. "Taylith, I don't understand any of this. I can't be your lifemate. I don't even want a serious relationship with *anyone*. I tried that once and it didn't go well."

He was surprised at that information. "What happened?"

"I don't like to think about it, much less tell anyone. I'll tell you in one sentence. I was left at the altar."

"Laura, I—"

"Please? No more. I hope you understand now why I don't want to be involved. We were probably in our spaceships for a long time, but to me it's still like it happened yesterday."

Even though he had known she did not share his feelings, it still hurt to hear her voice them. He caressed her cheek. "You do not have to accept the bond. Both lifemates must agree to complete a joining."

Suddenly an agonizing pain speared through him, spreading outward, through his limbs, his joints, his bones. He knew that feeling. It had happened once before, centuries ago when Cewrick had cast his spell. The change had begun. "Run, Laura. Now!"

She stood there shaking her head, her blonde hair flying around her shoulders. "I am not going anywhere."

Gods, the woman is stubborn.

"You...need...to...leave..." His knees hit the ground, the pain engulfing him.

She kneeled on the ground in front of him and placed her arms around his neck. "I might be really pissed off at you right now, but I sure as hell am not leaving you to deal with this on your own. Friends don't do that, Taylith. They stick by each other."

Exasperated, he brushed her hair away from her face. *Gods, she was an obstinate woman.* "You have to step back. I don't want to crush you."

A look of understanding crossed her features. She nodded, stood up, and gave him some room. Through a haze of pain, he vaguely noticed the others gathered around them. He returned his focus to Laura. Gods, the determined wench. He had to keep her safe. Losing track of his surroundings, he allowed the beast to emerge.

Wispy black smoke snaked its way around his reptilian body. He spied the others through the film of fog holding Laura by the arms to keep her from running to him. She broke free of their hands and raced to him. He lowered his head and allowed her to climb onto his back.

Suddenly, the curling black mist turned into a vortex swirling around them. He placed a shield around his precious cargo, ensuring Laura stayed seated upon his back. Then he spread his wings, letting the wind carry them to the realm of the Blood Lagoon. She lay forward against his neck, her arms and legs hugging him tightly, her fingers gripping his scales. He knew she was frightened, but he could feel the fierce determination emanating from her. The vision had shown it was Laura who had to retrieve the key. He prayed to the gods that it was true.

Inky blackness gave way to an eerie red sky. The red tint of the clouds was caused by the reflection of the lake of blood below. Taylith glided over the area, raining fire on the monstrous creatures that drank from the water's edge. He landed after finding a large enough area for his dragon's body, then kneeled to allow Laura to slide down to the ground.

He nudged her with his nose. *I am sorry the gods require this of you. The key is in the center of the lagoon, resting upon a rock far below the surface of the water.*

She brushed her fingers across the scales of his neck. "I would do anything to save my sister, Taylith. Even if it costs me my life."

We must do this quickly. I will keep the beasts away from the lagoon. But, Laura, be careful please...even of me. I do not know how much power Zohmes will have over me if he decides to use the other half of my soul shard.

"I'll swim as fast as I can." She pulled the pendant from beneath her shirt and held his soul shard in her hand. The crystal began to glow, enveloping her in a bright shield of light. Taylith watched as she turned to enter the poisonous water.

He scanned their surroundings while she swam. Huge crags of rock surrounded the crater lake. Some had cavernous holes large enough for the black dragons he had seen in his vision to hide inside. Many of the creatures that resided in the realm were in their lairs or waiting below the surface. He spread his wings and leaped into the air, gliding around the lake, guarding Laura as she swam. She was surprisingly fast and in a blink of an eye dove below the surface of the water in search of the key. Before long she surfaced, spitting and sputtering. Her beautiful honey-blonde hair and her face were covered in the blood-red liquid. He kept his vigil in the sky while she hurriedly swam to the bank of the lagoon. When she found footing, she waded the rest of the way to the edge.

He landed at the edge of the water when she had safely reached the bank. The red water covered her like paint, dripping from her clothing, forming a river of bloody water beneath her feet as she walked toward him. She held the key triumphantly above her head.

"I did it! The stuff didn't kill me! Let's go save my sister!"

His gaze turned upward as the beat of large wings echoed around them. Black scales glinted in the sky. A group of at least ten dragons flew toward them at high speed. He kneeled to allow Laura to climb onto his back. *Climb on quickly. I can fight them easier in the sky, and I will not leave you on the ground without protection.*

After she was safely on his back, he spread his wings, but it was too late to take flight. Several of the dragons hovered above and three landed on the ground in front of them. He snapped his wings back, lest they tried to ground him, and released a rumbling growl. He had no wish to engage them in a fight or wound any of them, but he would if he had to. The creatures were lost jewel dragons, still bound by the curse. The largest of the dragons took a step toward them, its head lowered. It chuffed as it scented the air. The dragons above them dispersed to fly above the lagoon. The last three spread their wings and lunged into the air to follow their retreating brethren.

Taylith wondered why the black dragons had not attacked the invaders of their territory. After Cewrick was defeated, all the jewel dragons had their shards restored to them. Why did these dragons not receive theirs? He knew now they were placed here to protect the lagoon. Could they be bound to it, like Ciara had been bound to the Clyss? Where were their soul shards? Or were these just ordinary dragons, creatures created by Zohmes?

A loud crack of thunder rent the air. A bright light flashed in the sky. Clouds swirled in the center, illuminated by a green glow. A distorted voice sounded in his mind, then cleared to Ciara's as the glowing vortex grew larger. *Taylith...please. Can you hear me? Something is stopping us from reaching you.*

He surged into the air, flying straight for the clouds. *Ciara. Don't try to come through, but whatever spell you are using, don't stop.*

Chanting sounded from below, not Ciara's voice but something more sinister. Taylith scanned the ground beneath them to find the source. Beside the lagoon stood a figure, ropes of magic issuing from his fingertips, a chant whispering from his lips, growing in volume like a raging storm. *Odoxon.* The sorcerer grasped a pendant around his neck. It began to shine brightly, first a soft golden glow, then changing colors to a sickly green. Taylith's wings faltered, his great reptilian body seizing with pain, suddenly plunging steadily from the sky. His mind clouded, his consciousness receded. Taylith knew then the sorcerer had kept his soul shard instead of releasing it to Zohmes.

"Taylith! Do something... Oh God!" Laura screamed, one hand holding tightly to his scales.

Her call pulsed through his soul, their connection flaring to life as he sensed her grabbing his soul shard and holding it. He was her guardian and he could allow no harm to come to her. He fought the pain, spread his wings, and managed to stop their downward plummet. He soared through the air, then circled above Odoxon. Taylith pulled in a deep rumbling breath, then rained fire below him, hoping to incinerate the sorcerer. It was of little use. Odoxon shielded himself, but it kept him busy enough for Taylith to take advantage.

Spotting the swirling vortex ahead of him, he shot toward it at high speed, breaking through the whirlwind of clouds and climbing steadily into the air to above the Dreaded Peaks.

CHAPTER SIX

Snow fell even heavier once he had crossed the craggy, sharp peaks. To his surprise, the suns were just starting to set and hung low in the winter sky. When they had gone to the Blood Lagoon, it was late at night. He dove to fly between the ridges and spotted the temple easily. Carved from black rock, the temple stood as a stark contrast against the white snow that blanketed the mountaintops. The shrine and towers were rigid like the shards of mountain that surrounded them. A sconce holding a blazing torch had been mounted on each side of the metal door Evior had described, lighting up the area. Evil-looking guards holding long pikes stood on each side.

Taylith made sure to fly high enough so they would not see him. *Do you see it, Laura?*

"Yes, I do. Aren't you going to kill those two monstrous-looking dudes? We need to get into that temple now that I have the key."

Ssh. Talk in your mind, Laura. I can hear you, just like you can hear me. No, I cannot kill them now. That would alert Zohmes and Odoxon.

"Weren't you just talking to me?"

Yes, in your mind. You are holding part of my soul shard, so I can communicate with you in this way.

"Okay… I'd better watch what I think, then."

I said, think it, do not speak. We do not want them to hear us. We need to get back to the team.

Are you able to change back to your human?

I think so. We will find out once we get back.

This is so cool. I heard you earlier but thought it was my imagination working overtime. I've heard of telepathy but never thought it was real.

It is between some. Not everyone has the ability.

The temple looks creepy.

Yes. And from what Evior described, it is worse behind that door.

He sped up again and soared high, rising above the peaks. It did not take him long to reach the campsite. He landed near the edge of the forest, allowed Laura to slide down, then commanded her to step back. Concentrating hard, he changed into his human, but it caused a lot of pain. For now, his jewel dragon was gone. All he had was the black dragon. But at least he still had his humanity, which surprised him. Something was very different. Could Astiana have been correct? That splitting his soul shard would protect him as well? Gods, he hoped it did. With Zohmes and Odoxon in possession of half his shard, the risk was there of him being turned completely. If he lost his humanity, their mission would fail. *But Laura had managed to stop the sorcerer's spell by clasping the shard she wore.*

The team had seen him land and shift and hurried toward them. "Taylith, Laura, I am glad to see you both back in one piece." Ciara hugged him tightly. "You have been gone almost a day."

"We felt helpless," Erica added.

Astiana held out a blanket for Laura. "Young lady, we need to get you cleaned up somehow. You look like you have stepped out of a bucket of red paint."

46

Taylith managed a chuckle. "She has the key."

Laura poked her arm out of the blanket and held it up. "Here it is."

Taylith watched the women help Laura clean herself. The women had melted snow over the fire, so she was able to cleanse herself properly, even rinse the red goo out of her hair. When Ciara went to take the chain and shard off, Laura stopped her. "No! Leave it."

It warmed his heart a little to know she was not completely rejecting his soul shard. Then he realized they were all in grave danger from Odoxon and Zohmes. By now, Zohmes would know that Laura had the key and that Odoxon had not been able to get the other half of his shard. Unless this was all part of the big plan. He needed to talk to Ciara or Astiana, but right now, they were busy with Laura.

"Icaras, Cewrick, we need a shield around the campsite. Now," he told them. "Zohmes and Odoxon will be furious that Laura retrieved the key."

Astiana returned and sat next to Taylith. "I do not think they will do anything. This is a plan that has been set in motion. They want you and Laura to enter the temple."

Taylith frowned. "What plan? Why would they want us to enter the temple?"

Astiana patted his knee. "I am not sure, but Zohmes and Odoxon have the other half of your soul shard. They will want the half in Laura's possession as well."

He clenched his jaw and gave Astiana a pointed stare. "That will never happen. I would crush it before I allowed them to take it from Laura." If he destroyed his soul shard, he would be released to the realm of dreams, or so the legends had said. It was not something he had ever witnessed. No dragon willingly destroyed their soul shard, but if the stories were true, it would put him out of Zohmes and Odoxon's reach as well as protect Laura and the team.

"No! You will not, Taylith! I forbid it!" Ciara sat on the ground in front of him, concern clouding her features.

"That is not your choice, Ciara. You do not live with the horrors that haunt my dreams, and I will not allow myself to be enslaved again," he said vehemently.

"But what you are thinking is not an option. You have gifted Laura with half of your shard. It is rightfully hers and she will never give it up." Ciara stood and returned to sit closer to the fire next to Brenn.

Laura joined him, clutching the blanket around her. She moved closer to the fire, so he shifted forward, too.

"Laro and Erica are drying my clothes with their fleet weapons. Now what is this I caught about your shard?"

"Nothing for you to concern yourself with."

"You don't have to worry. I won't let anyone or anything take this from my neck, Taylith." She poked a hand out of the blanket and patted his leg reassuringly.

Erica plopped down on the ground beside Laura and handed her a bundle of dry clothing. "Thanks, Erica. I almost hate getting out of this warm blanket."

Laura left and returned quickly, dressed in her dry clothing. She sat on the ground beside him and leaned her head against his shoulder, snuggling up against him, her body shivering. "I can't believe how cold it is getting."

Taylith put his arm around her and pulled her closer to his side. "Winters are very harsh in Sirona, especially near the Dreaded Peaks."

Ivran, Laro, and Icaras had gathered more wood and piled it on the fire. It was blazing now and giving them a lot of heat.

The temperature had dropped steadily after the suns had set, and snow fell continually from the darkened sky. A breeze began driving the freezing snow into their faces, so they all moved closer to the fire, huddling together to stay warm.

The fire sparked and crackled, and the flames flickering in the wind rose quite high now, blanketing the area in warmth and keeping the snow at bay.

Taylith pulled his coat off and placed it around Laura's shoulders. "We should move our tents closer to the fire."

"Yes, good plan," Brenn agreed as he and Ivran stood. Just as they were about to start on moving their tents, the flames seemed to get out of control, shooting high in the sky and sending sparks flying in the wind. A form began to materialize in the flames, then slowly rose above the fire.

"Izarus," Astiana and Ciara both exclaimed.

His long, white hair drifted in the breeze around his ageless face. Piercing eyes gazed at them. The deep tenor of his voice boomed and echoed around the camp. "I have been sent to you by the creator, I Am. Zohmes and Odoxon have angered him with the evil they have sown on Ierilia. I Am has enlisted the help of all gods and goddesses to aid you in your quest to defeat them. Dreaded Peaks and its valley were once called the Astanica Mountains, and Astanica Valley."

Astiana gasped and exclaimed, "That was my home!"

Izarus sent her a frowning stare. "The temple you seek was Astiana's temple of worship. It was beautiful once, the mountains and valley verdant with vegetation and flowers. After Zohmes banished Astiana and turned her into a statue, he began his rule of terror on Ierilia. But only until Rithar bound Zohmes to Yanata. When Zohmes escaped Yanata, he returned to Astanica Valley. He changed the temple to suit his needs. He altered the appearance of the mountains and the valley, and he created Blood Lagoon, once called Shimmering Basin. It was very similar to the Clyss and had magical qualities, as you must remember, Astiana."

49

"What happened to the people in the valley? The farmers?" Astiana asked.

"Zohmes bound them to him. Beware. He and Odoxon have created an army of hybrids using the innocent farmers and their families. Not only here, but all over Ierilia. He will use anyone to further his means. He and the sorcerer are gathering that army to one location. He has also infiltrated the Yeavoth who have turned against the king. All of Ierilia is in grave danger. War threatens. Zohmes will stop at nothing to once again become ruler of Ierilia."

"Izarus, we must first rescue Julia and Niqine before we can deal with anything else. They are in Zohmes and Odoxon's clutches." Astiana stood while she spoke to the imposing figure.

Izarus frowned again, showing his displeasure at the interruptions. "Zohmes wants Laura so he can use her to control Julia, who carries the child. Once you rescue the young woman, Rania will take her to a safe place where Zohmes and Odoxon cannot find her. She will give birth there and remain until all is safe. Do not fear the child. It has Zohmes' essence in his blood, but also Julia's. Without Zohmes' influence, the infant will lead a normal life.

"You face grave danger when entering the valley of the Dreaded Peaks and the temple. Biryn, I have strengthened your powers, so you can assist the others. Much magick will be needed for you all to defeat those that rule the temple. Do not fear. We are with you. Taylith, look before you on the ground."

Taylith tore his gaze away from Izarus and looked at the ground. Before him, sparkling in the flames of the fire, lay the other half of his soul shard.

"I have restored your shard to you. Odoxon and Zohmes no longer have power over the black dragon. Now that you have your shard, you are again the jewel dragon you were meant to be. Your quest begins tomorrow. Sleep well, my children. I have placed a shield around your camp to safeguard you from predators. I must leave you now."

Izarus' snow-white hair flew around his head as he slowly ascended upward, then disappeared.

Taylith picked up his shard, thankful that the god had returned it to him.

Laura brushed her hand against his, touching the shard he held. The crystal glowed brightly beneath her fingertips. "Can it be put back together?"

Astiana smiled. "Of course, child. I will fuse them back together."

Taylith and Laura gave Astiana both halves of the soul shard. She closed her hand around them, chanting softly. Within moments her words ceased and in her palm lay the repaired soul shard, still set as a pendant with the gold chain. Taylith was relieved when Laura took the shard from Astiana and placed it back around her neck.

"Thank you, Astiana." Taylith studied the group of people tasked with keeping Ierilia safe. Each one would lay down their lives to protect the planet and its people. "I was shown the army in my vision. They will not be easy to defeat."

Astiana's eyes glistened with tears. "Defeating evil has never been an easy task. I am heartsick that Dreaded Peaks was once my realm, the place where Zohmes and I first lived and from where he ruled Ierilia. It was beautiful and peaceful, until the darkness in Zohmes' soul began to rule him."

"When did the rulers move to Cront?" Taylith asked.

"I am not sure. The palace in Cront has been the seat of the crown for many centuries. Maybe after Zohmes was banished, Rithar did not want to be reminded of everything that happened. It must be recorded in history which king built the first palace in Cront."

"The thought of war disturbs me," Brenn said, frowning.

Erica nodded. "Yes, and with the Yeavoth involved? Those giants and their fucking big gorillas? Could prove interesting."

Laura's eyebrows shot up. "Gorillas?"

Erica snickered. "You've got no idea, Laura. You saw *Star Wars*. Picture the Wookie and you see Yeavoth's warriors."

"Enough banter for this evening. We all have much to think about," Aldis said. "Let us bed down for the night. We leave early in the morning for the temple."

CHAPTER SEVEN

Taylith waited until Laura crept into her tent, then went to his own. The shield around the camp and the roaring fire kept the area quite warm. The snow had melted to just beyond the tents. He crawled into his bedroll, closed his eyes, and tried not to think about what Izaras had said. A rustling sound at the front of his tent startled him from his thoughts. He snatched his fleet weapon where it lay beside him, sitting up he pointed the gun at the tent opening.

A glimmer stick lit up the tent, and Laura stepped through the flaps.

He lowered his weapon and cast her a worried glance. "Laura? Woman, I was ready to shoot whatever creature was trying to get into my tent. Are you all right?"

She nodded, her blonde hair bouncing around her shoulders. "Yes." She glanced at him and scrunched up her face. "I really don't want to be alone, Taylith. Can I sleep here?"

He shifted his body over and motioned for her to join him. "Of course. You did not bring your bedroll?"

Laura shrugged and smiled. "I figured there's enough room in yours for both of us. Besides, you are warm and it's freaking cold."

He waited until she crawled in beside him, then took her into his arms. She sighed and snuggled up against him, laying her head on his shoulder.

"I'm scared, Taylith."

"No need to be afraid."

She peeked up at him. "You heard what Izarus said. Julia is to be whisked away to some secret place where I won't even be able to visit her or be with her when she gives birth. And war?"

He stroked her damp hair. "Ierilia's problems are far from over. Do not worry about Julia. Maybe the gods will find another solution."

"Will the problems ever stop?"

"Gods, Laura, I do not know. I try not to ponder on what the future holds." The visions had shown him quite enough, and a future without Laura was not something he wished to contemplate. It felt so good to hold her in his arms.

"Taylith, I know now what lifemate means. You gave me your soul shard. But though I don't want to give it back to you, I am not ready for a serious relationship. I hope you understand."

"I am trying to. You told me your betrothed left you at the altar. Can you tell me about it?" He heard her deep sigh. If she did not want to talk about it, he would not pressure her.

"I have feelings for you. Much more than I care to admit to, but the pain Ryan caused me is still so fresh in my mind. He was my first love. We were engaged, promised to each other. The date of the wedding, the joining, was all set for two weeks prior to our departure, and everything was arranged. On the day of our wedding, he never showed up at the church. There was another wedding that afternoon and the priest finally asked us to leave. It was the most horrible moment of my life. Julia came through for me. She told the guests there would be no wedding. Ryan also left the program. He joined because of me and was accepted, but was never happy about it. I still wonder if his crazy act was some sort of rebellion against me and the relocation mission."

"Did you ever find out the truth of it all?"

"Yes. His best friend, who was also his attendant, came and told me. Ryan had run off with one of my friends, Gail, and hastily married her in Las Vegas. Apparently, they had been having an affair for a while. In other words, he had been sleeping with her and betrayed me."

Taylith pulled her tighter into his arms and kissed the top of her head. "Then he was unfaithful, and it was not an act of rebellion against you and the mission. I am so sorry. You need never be afraid of me. If a dragon gives their soul shard to their destined lifemate, that dragon is already bound, heart and soul. To break that bond would be a sacrilege and the gods would take my soul shard away from me as punishment."

But what would happen should their lifemate choose to return it, or worse, keep the shard but refuse to complete the bond? Taylith had never heard of such a thing happening. The idea of it was not something he wished to think about. Though he knew that even if Laura were not his lifemate, he would have given her his soul shard. Even before he had realized she was his lifemate, she had captured him heart and soul.

"Give me time, Taylith?"

"You can have all the time you need, Laura. Now sleep. Tomorrow we need to be strong and alert." He pecked her on the cheek, then waited until her steady breathing told him she slept.

Thanks to the shield Izarus had placed around them, the

night passed without incident. All were awake early. When Taylith opened his eyes, his arms were empty. Laura had already left the tent. Of course. She was anxious to rescue her sister.

Due to the cold, they had slept in their clothing. Taylith hurried to relieve himself, then joined the team by the fire. "Morning, everyone. Thank you, Izarus, for a quiet night!"

Laura handed him a stick with roasted meat on it and a chunk of bread. The fire still burned, though not as high as the night before. "Thank you." He sank to the ground next to her. "You slept well, Laura?"

"Yes, surprisingly well after yesterday's adventure."

Taylith quickly ate his meat and his bread, then drank the tea Ciara handed him. "Like I told you last night, we cannot go to that valley in the hovercraft. There is no place to land it. There are sharp metal protrusions as tall as a man that are close together throughout the whole valley, from beginning to end. Zohmes probably placed them there."

"I never saw those," Laura said.

"My dragon's eyes can see far. The terrain is dangerous. But Ciara and I can fly us all. You just have to be careful when you slide off our backs to not land on one of those sharp spikes."

"But you won't be able to land there either," Erica pointed out.

"No, but we can hover just above. When we are ready to call out our humans, Astiana, Cewrick, and Icaras can bespell us to float above the spikes so we can touch ground safely."

Biryn stood and pulled on his warming gloves. "Time to go."

The men quickly doused the fire. "Do we leave the camp as it is?" Taylith asked.

"Yes. The shield Izarus created is still in place. We can

leave, return, but nothing else can penetrate his spell," Astiana answered.

They quickly gathered their weapons and followed Ciara and Taylith to an open area. Taylith had never felt more relieved as he changed into his jewel dragon, the black dragon hopefully gone forever.

He and Ciara kneeled to allow the team to climb onto their backs. As soon as everyone was settled and shielded, they lunged into the air and flew toward the Dreaded Peaks. The dragons flew swiftly, and it did not take them long to reach the snow-covered crags and peaks. The sharp metal spikes cut through the layer of snow below, the knife-edged points making it impossible for them to land.

Taylith scanned the mountaintops as they flew, looking for the temple hidden within the barbed crests. He spotted it easily, just as he had the day before. The black of the temple stood out starkly against the white snow on the ground. He led Ciara to an area where there was enough space between the metal protrusions, so that they could safely allow their riders to slide to the ground. After everyone had two feet planted firmly on the snow, Astiana, Cewrick, and Icaras shielded Taylith and Ciara so they could shift mid-air and descend to the ground as their humans.

But as soon as their feet hit the surface, the jagged metal spikes came alive. The blades of metal shuffled and moved, the ground rumbled. The metal glowed and shifted into huge creatures. Pointed metal spikes covered their stocky bodies of metal armor. They had large steel plates protecting their backs and heads, four red eyes, and a large mouth with rows of shiny needle-like fangs. Huge metal pinchers protruded from their arms, and their legs split into four pointed feet.

"Use your shields," Astiana shouted.

"Laura! Where are you?" Taylith drew his sword and

swiveled in a circle. He tried to catch a glimpse of her, but the creatures advanced so quickly, they obstructed his view. Fear pierced his soul. He could not find her among the mass of bodies. Unlike the rest of the team, Laura was not gifted with the power to protect herself with magick. He breathed a sigh of relief when he spotted her. Erica stood beside her, sword at the ready. Light enveloped her like at the Blood Lagoon, providing a protective shield around her body, the power within him safeguarding her against the creatures advancing upon them.

Laura raised her proton phaser and joined Ivran, Laro, and Aldis firing their weapons at the vermin. The weapons did little to wound the abominations. They hissed and bristled their bodies, the metal protrusions rising from their backs and sides, deflecting the beams from the firearms.

One of the monsters lunged at Taylith. He thrust his sword deep within its body between the metal spikes. It glowed a fierce red and melted into a puddle of bubbling steel. "Use your swords," he shouted, and one by one, he jabbed and plunged his blade into the beasts. A river of liquid metal flowed, melting the ice and snow. But the creatures kept coming. There were too many of them and only four of them had the swords that could destroy the monstrosities.

Cewrick raised his staff into the air, a spell issuing from his lips. Rays of lightning blasted from the jeweled top, illuminating the sky above them, high enough to not touch the humans. The monstrosities froze, literally turning into ice. Taylith pulled his arm from a claw that had solidified around it. The massive appendage crumbled, the rest of the body slowly following. Thousands of icy particles rained down as one after the other the metal monsters disintegrated.

"Is everyone all right?" Aldis yelled, his voice echoing through the valley.

Everyone mumbled their assent while gathering their supplies and shouldering their packs.

Taylith grabbed Laura's hand. It did not matter if his soul shard protected her—an uncommon occurrence—he would not lose sight of her again. "Now to the temple."

Progress was slow as they trudged forward in the knee-deep snow. The skin suits they wore beneath their clothing helped to keep the frigid cold at bay, but the wind drove sheets of falling snow into their faces, fogging their view.

"What the hell! You guys design the ultimate pair of long johns, but you don't have snowshoes? Damn, I'd give anything for a pair of snowshoes right now! At least my feet would stay above the snow," Laura complained while forcefully moving her body forward.

"I would kill for a pair of snowshoes. If this crud gets any deeper, I'm going to drown in it," Erica grumbled.

Taylith glanced at Erica. The woman was as small as a youngling and built just as delicate. What she lacked in height and build, she made up for in ferocity and skill. Biryn had chosen well when he had gifted her the fourth sword.

After what had seemed like hours, the black structure of the temple loomed before them. They stopped their progress and hid behind an outcropping of rocks and ice to keep from being spotted by the guards.

Taylith studied the temple and its immediate grounds. "Two guards were posted at the entrance when I flew over the temple yesterday. I could see no other way in or out of the structure, but there are probably tunnels that lead out of the temple."

"Unless the guards are blind as a bat, they can see that the valley is devoid of their cute robo creatures," Erica remarked. "They'll be alerted, for sure."

The massive carved temple stood as an omen to those that

dared to cross Zohmes. The priests within, devout to Zohmes, had risked everything to free him from Yanata, including the sacrifice of innocent blood on an altar of evil. It sickened Taylith to think of the ritual Evior had described to them.

Taylith pointed out the entrance and the hideous guards posted on either side of the huge metal door. "We will lose the element of surprise the moment we leave the shelter of these rocks."

The two monsters stood ready in front of the doors, turning their grotesque heads from side to side, their spears held out to pierce anyone attempting to enter.

Taylith stepped back as Cewrick took his place. His staff glowed while he mumbled a spell. In seconds, the two guards stood frozen in time.

"We can approach the door now," Cewrick told them.

They quickly advanced to the steel door. Like the metal creatures, the guards crumbled into hundreds of icy particles when touched by one of the swords. Taylith stood before the imposing threshold. Embedded in the door were strange symbols and etchings of faces and animals.

"This is nothing like the entrance to my temple of worship." Astiana gingerly touched the door.

Taylith fingered the large keyhole. "Laura, you need to unlock it."

Taking the key from her pocket, she joined him and handed him the key. Taylith inserted it. He did not need to turn it. As soon as he pushed it into its hole, the door began to slide upward into the cliff face. The key fell to the ground. Taylith bent to pick it up and stuck it in his pocket.

Weapons ready, they waited for it to almost fully open before hesitantly stepping inside. They faced a long hallway lit by sconces that hung on the walls. Nothing awaited them. The corridor was empty.

"I do not trust this," Biryn mumbled.

Taylith agreed. "They must know we are here."

Brenn called out as he headed the team, "Advance with caution. Have your weapons ready. Eyes front, back, left, and right."

Taylith made sure Laura was right beside him. He marveled at her ability and strength of will to contain her eagerness to reach her sister. The hallway was almost like a museum. Large windows dotted both walls. Behind the glass, statues of strange animals and even stranger people depicted various methods of torture. One scene illustrated a ritual. A young woman lay naked on a slab, a hooded figure hovering over her, a knife above her chest. When he placed his hand on the glass, he withdrew it quickly. It was not glass. It was a sheet of clear ice.

Laura grasped his hand. "Do you think those were once real people?"

"None is real. It is all illusion, meant to scare us off," Astiana told them.

The corridor seemed endless. They finally emerged into the cavern Evior had described. Its walls were craggy. Red slime flowed steadily as if the mountain oozed blood. More than a hundred, from what Taylith could see, black-cloaked figures knelt on the floor, their hoods drawn up over their heads. The altar stood at the far back with dozens of lit black candles on it. The altar seemed carved from black marble and glowed a fiery red. The same strange symbols they had seen on the door had been etched into its front. An urn stood in the center between two gold candelabras with burning black candles. Red-robed priests stood behind the altar, their cowls drawn over their heads, hiding their faces. Each held a red staff topped by a black skull.

In front of the altar was a stone, sacrificial slab. On it lay a naked young woman, her blonde hair spilling over the sides of the table.

"Oh my God! That is Julia!" Laura hissed.

A red-cloaked figure stood beside the table, a knife poised over the young woman's abdomen.

"Calm yourself, Laura," Ciara told her from behind. "That is not Julia. It is another illusion. Zohmes would not kill the infant."

"If it isn't Julia, then who is it?"

"Maybe there is nothing there," Astiana said.

"If it's another young woman appearing to be Julia, we have to rescue her," Laura told them.

They stood behind the kneeling worshippers. As if on cue, the cloaked figures jumped up and turned. Taylith drew his sword, his proton phaser in his other hand. "Get behind me, Laura!" he shouted.

The horde attacked. Skeletal faces emerged from the cowls, animalistic faces, deformed faces, all Zohmes' creations and all bound to the evil god. The team fought in a line, slowly annihilating one creature after the other, but as fast as they killed their attackers, others emerged. There seemed to be hundreds more advancing toward them.

Taylith watched helplessly as Laura pushed her way forward through the throng of attackers, bravely killing those in her path. A glow surrounded her. *My shard? Is it still protecting her?* He tried to follow but was thwarted each time.

Cewrick wielded his magick, but another force stopped the streams of fire issuing from his wand. "Zohmes and Odoxon are blocking my magick!" he shouted.

Taylith could barely see Laura anymore through the throng of attackers. He finally glimpsed her advancing to the sacrificial table and saw her kill the robed figure holding the knife. The priests behind the altar rushed forward and removed the young woman from the table, then grabbed Laura. They disappeared with both women.

"Nooooooo!" Taylith shouted. He threw himself into the throng of fighting adversaries and fought beside his team mates. Inner fury drove him on, annihilating anything that was in his path. He made it to the altar but saw no entrance, no way to follow Laura. Where had they taken her? Who was the other young woman? Ciara had said it was not Julia, that it was an illusion causing them to see Julia.

The wall behind the altar glowed a bright red and almost seemed liquid. Suddenly, a face appeared. It was a hideous face surrounded by flaming red hair, wild eyes, and the most nefarious grin he had ever seen. Horrendous laughter echoed throughout the cavern. It seemed to fuel the creatures attacking them. Taylith stood right before the altar now, ignoring the face and the hideous laughter. For some reason, the urn drew him to it. The urn looked the same as the one he had been shown in the vision. It was important. He had to get it.

Something came at him from behind. He swiveled just in time to kill his attacker. He turned back to the urn and grabbed it. Backing away toward the liquid red wall, clutching the urn under his arm, he fell through it into another cavern.

"Your friends will soon join you," a harsh voice told him.

Taylith swiveled. It was Odoxon. "You bastard! What have you done with Laura?" Through his worry and anguish he noticed he had picked up on some of the Earth language and smiled wryly.

"She is where we want her. With her sister. And now that we have you, we can keep both under control."

Taylith could hardly stand to be so close to the old sorcerer. "My friends will rescue us."

Another figure appeared beside Odoxon. It was Zohmes. "You would put the mother of your child through all this?" Taylith asked.

"Julia is safe and well. Her sister is by her side, which has made her more than happy. They are comfortable and will be well cared for."

"And what do you intend to do with me?"

"Without your soul shard you are nothing. Laura has the shard. She has not yet given it up, but she will. For now, Laura realizes that if she does not comply, you will suffer. We will grant her a vision of your confinement."

Before Taylith realized, he found himself in a cave with a barred door. He wondered about the rest of the team. Were they still fighting off the horde? Why did Cewrick's magick not work? Maybe it was because he could not link with Ciara, Astiana, Icaras, and Biryn. He recalled when they had rescued Hirsuta, Cewrick had needed to be linked to one of them.

Oh, Rania, Izarus, gods and goddesses, if you can hear me, please help?

He looked helplessly around the barren cave. Small vermin scurried along the stone floor. More than anything, he wished now that he had his own magick, that he could just whisk himself out of there. But when he had been released from Cewrick's curse, the magick he had been born with had not returned.

CHAPTER EIGHT

How could he have fallen asleep? Unless it was another spell placed upon him. He sat up groggily. When his eyes became accustomed to the dim light, he noticed his team mates. He counted them. They were all there. Except for Laura. Gods, he hoped she was safe. She had to be. If Zohmes and Odoxon managed to get his soul shard from her, she would have no protection against them.

Remembering the urn, he patted the floor around him, searching for it. He breathed a sigh of relief when his hand touched the cold metal. Zohmes and Odoxon had not taken it. He pulled the lid off and looked inside. He could not believe the priests had been stupid enough to leave the urn out in the open. His heart pounding, he reached his hand inside and touched the soul shards nestled safely inside and counted them. Ten. There were ten dragons bound to Blood Lagoon. Who could they be? They had lost so many over the centuries.

Unsteadily, he stood and went to Brenn and Ciara. "Brenn...Ciara, wake up."

"Huh? Where am I?" Brenn sat up and brushed his hair out of his eyes.

"In a cave somewhere deep beneath the temple." Taylith

handed the urn to Ciara when she managed to pull herself up beside Brenn.

Ciara looked inside and gasped. "Whose are they? I thought all of us were free."

"I think they belong to the black dragons trapped at Blood Lagoon. We can free them if they are theirs, but for now we need to hide the shards."

Ciara placed a protective spell on the urn and shoved it inside her backpack. "I will keep them safe."

Taylith looked at Brenn. "How did all of you get trapped here?"

Brenn shook his head. "There were hundreds of Zohmes' minions. We fought so hard. It seemed each time we killed a bunch, more would come. Just as they did at Feared Peaks. Zohmes and Odoxon must have used their combined magick to transport us here."

"They have Laura. I could not get through the mob of vermin in time to save her from the priests. She is with Julia, and Zohmes told me they have threatened her that they will torture me if she does not comply with their demands."

The rest of the team began to wake. "Where am I?" Biryn asked, looking around with a dazed expression.

Cewrick stood up and brushed dirt from his clothing. "We're confined below the temple. Now that we are all together, we can fight Odoxon and Zohmes. It was near impossible with that throng of miscreations attacking us."

Icaras stepped to his father's side. "We need to see if we can transport all of us out of here. Everyone get in a circle and join hands."

They formed a circle and the magick users began to chant. A wind blew in the cave, swirling around them and picking up speed, then eventually dying down and dissipating. The spell did not work.

Frustrated, Taylith pulled his hand free and walked to the barred door, examining the lock and frame. The frame had the same strange symbols etched into it as the entry to the temple. "We have to figure a way out of this dungeon. Zohmes and Odoxon would not have dropped us here if they knew we could just chant a spell and escape."

Erica walked up beside him and touched one of the symbols. "Of course not. Zohmes and Doxie wouldn't make it that easy. What are these? They kind of look like what we call a ward on Earth."

Taylith raised a brow. Doxie? She had given the sorcerer a pet name? He would have at least picked one of the other Earth terms like asshole, or bastard. "What is a ward?"

Erica brushed her fingers through her unruly curls. "There are some on Earth that believe they can use magic. They use symbols for different things, like for protection...or to keep demons and other evil beings trapped."

Sometimes Erica's Earth terms made sense. Taylith stuck his hand in his pocket and pulled the key out that Laura had retrieved from the Blood Lagoon. "I think I have our way out." He held the key up for the others to see.

"That's the key you used to open the entrance door," Erica said. "How can it work here?"

"You all missed the hole. See this octagon opening in the center of this symbol? The key will fit in it." He promptly inserted the key and the barred door slid open. Two hideous guards jumped up immediately, advancing toward them, spears leveled at the prisoners.

Cewrick aimed his staff at the two grotesque figures. Taylith felt a shiver run down his spine. They could hardly be called men. Their elongated heads had a row of tiny beady eyes from top to bottom, glowing with a menacing green light. Deformed faces with a mouth resembling that of a skeleton, with large, sharp, brown teeth. Large pointy ears reached to over the top of the skulls. They were twice as tall, towering over the humans. They wore some kind of insane uniform, undoubtedly another Zohmes creation. Red with gold braid trimmed all down the front and the sleeves. Their feet resembled claws. Their giant hands only had three fingers. Taylith had taken all this in in seconds, before Cewrick turned the two guards into small piles of ashes.

"We need to find Laura and Julia." Taylith scanned the corridor. Several cells lined the wall, all barred with doors framed by the strange symbols. The cells appeared to be empty except one. "It is the young woman they had on the sacrificial table. She was real. They just made her look like Julia. I will not leave her to be tortured and killed."

"Not to forget Niqine." Icaras strode up to them.

The young woman, her long, brown hair disheveled, crouched in a corner. She looked at them, her brown eyes large and scared. "Do not be afraid. Come with us. We are here to rescue our friends. Where are you from?" Taylith carefully approached her.

"My name is Zandria. I am from Wildevein. They plan to sacrifice me."

"We will return you to your home. Come. We must hurry." Taylith held his hand out. Zandria hesitantly took it and stood. She wore nothing but some kind of sack and shivered. He led her out of the dungeon to Ciara.

Brenn joined Cewrick. "You are with me. You can do the most damage with your staff. Icaras, you, Astiana, Biryn, and Ciara behind us, in case you need to join hands with Cewrick. The rest of you bring up the rear with Aldis."

After they had all left the dungeon, Taylith closed the door. "Just in case." He quickly joined the others.

"I will create an illusion of us. If anyone comes to check on us, they will think we are still in captivity. I will also create an illusion of the two guards." Cewrick raised his staff and mumbled foreign words.

When Taylith glanced through the bars, it seemed indeed as if they were all still there, unconscious, or sleeping on the ground. The two guards looked almost real.

"How long will this spell last?" Taylith wondered.

Cewrick waved his staff impatiently. "As long as I want it to last, or at least until we escape this place."

"This is nothing like my temple." Astiana sighed.

"I'm sorry." Erica placed a hand on Astiana's arm.

"Thank you, child."

Taylith waited for Brenn to take the initiative, but Brenn was hesitant. "Which way do we go? This tunnel leads both ways."

Ciara held up her hand. "Allow me a few moments?" She moved away from them and seemed in deep meditation. Taylith knew she was communicating with Rania. When she returned, she turned to him.

"Taylith, Rania told me you need to concentrate on Laura. She has your soul shard and can hear you. She may be able to guide us."

"That is if she remembers where they took her. I will try." He closed his eyes and called out to her.

Laura, can you hear me? Laura...Laura...answer me if you can.
Nothing happened. He tried again.

Laura, please. Hear my voice. Where are you? Can you hear me?
They all swiveled as a commotion sounded from the tunnel. Four guards, dressed in the same ridiculous costumes as the two Cewrick had killed, advanced toward them. Cewrick ran forward, his staff aimed straight at them. Their spears came dangerously close to his chest, but his staff and spell were faster.

Taylith? I hear you, but faintly. I am locked in a bedroom with Julia. Niqine is in the next room. I don't know how to show you the way. I don't remember. All I remember is them ushering me up some stairs.

We are here, and we will find you. Are you all right?

Yes, I'm fine. So is Julia. Taylith, I had to tell her...she...

The communication faded. "Laura answered me. She said she is in a bedroom and Niqine is in the room next to theirs. They took her up some stairs."

"So there are more layers to this temple. We will march on ahead first," Brenn decided.

"Laura mentioned that Niqine is in the next room."

They began making their way through the passage. "There have to be stairs somewhere," Brenn said.

"The temple is nothing like I remember it. I cannot guide you," Astiana told him.

"Are we going to the other side of the mountain?" Erica muttered. "This seems endless."

She had no sooner spoken, when Taylith spotted a door. Just like the others, it had the strange symbols on it. One of them had an octagon hole in the center. He dug the key out of his pocket and quickly inserted it. The door opened to a stone spiral staircase.

Taylith peered through the entry. There was no need to use glimmer sticks. The stairway was dimly lit by sconces embedded into the rock wall. The torches cast eerie shadows along the rockface. Sacrilegious symbols had been carved into the stone, winding up the walls along the stairs. Taylith averted his eyes from the pure evil etchings.

He stuck the key back into his pocket. "I have a feeling we are going to need this key to access any door we find."

Erica peered around his shoulder. "On Earth older houses and castles had one key that could unlock every door. They are called skeleton keys."

"Skeleton? As in made from skeleton bones?" Ivran questioned.

Erica giggled. "No. They were usually metal or bronze. It means that this one key could open every door in the place. It's just what it was called."

Taylith started up the steps, the others following in the same order as before. The narrow staircase seemed to go on forever. He was relieved to see the door looming in front of them. The door was the same as the one below. He pulled the key from his pocket and unlocked it, then carefully pushed it open. Cewrick stood behind him, his staff raised, ready to disintegrate Zohmes' minions should they happen upon them.

Taylith scanned both sides of the corridor. There were a lot of doors on each side of the long hallway, all of them steel, with markings etched upon them. It was like they were in a maze. The temple was huge, and they had no idea where the room was in which Laura was being held captive. He pulled the door closed enough to hide them. "The passageway is lined with doors on both sides. It is not feasible for us to check each room. I have to try to contact Laura again."

Laura, can you hear me? He waited, but there was no response. *Laura, answer me please?*

Taylith! Where are you?

We are in a corridor with a lot of doors. If you can give me a visual of the door you entered, it would help.

All I can tell you is that we went up some stairs, down a corridor, and then more stairs. The door to the room we are in had a lot of symbols on it. One stuck out at me. It was a big triangle, a skull in the center, and symbols around it.

What about the door leading to the stairs?

I don't remember. I'm sorry.

71

Honey, don't be sorry. You have helped. We are trying to find you. Stay strong.

Taylith told the others what Laura had said.

"So we have to find a door leading to another stairwell. She did not tell you anything about the door?" Brenn asked.

"No. Just that the door leading to where she is had the triangular etching on it."

Taylith opened the door a crack. No one in sight. "It seems clear."

"It's weird that Doxie and Zohmes haven't set their minions on us," Erica remarked.

Cewrick snorted. "I created the illusion of us in the dungeon. If they checked, they would think we are still there."

"Which door to the next stairs?" Astiana wondered.

They crept along the long corridor stealthily, but nothing stood in their way. One door seemed different from the others.

"Taylith, I think I see an octagon hole. Try inserting your key into it," Aldis called out.

Taylith hurried to the front and fished the key out of his pocket. He inserted it and the door opened, revealing another spiral staircase.

The staircase was much like the first one they had climbed. Taylith took the lead, knowing they would probably need the key to open the door leading into the next corridor above them. Finally reaching the door to the next corridor, he grabbed the key and unlocked the door. He pushed the door open and peered out.

"All is clear." He stepped into the hallway, the others following behind. "Quickly check the doors. We need to find the symbol Laura described."

They swiftly examined the doors on each side of the

passageway.

"I think I found it." Erica stopped in front of a large ornate door at the end of the hallway.

Taylith hurried to Erica's side. The door was larger than the others. Symbols were etched all the way around the frame, but what stood out was the symbol in the middle of the door, a large triangle with a skull in the center. The skull's mouth was open, and midpoint was the octagon keyhole.

The rest of the team gathered around them, ready to battle any minion that might come their way.

"The symbol is just as Laura described." He took the key and pushed it into the hole. Gods, he hoped they were right about it fitting all the doors. The longer it took to find Laura, the more likely their ruse would be found out. He held his breath and pushed the door open.

Julia shook her head and gazed up at Laura, tears running freely down her face. "No...no...no. Zohmes is a god. He said he had the power to bring John back, and he did. John is alive"

Laura brushed her hands through her hair and took a deep breath. Her sister could be so exasperating. She knew Julia was hurting. John was killed right in front of her. "Julia, how in the hell can you believe Zohmes and Odoxon! That creature you think is John is an illusion! It is Odoxon and Zohmes playing with your mind!"

"And how would you feel if Taylith were taken from you? I know you have feelings for him. I can see it." Julia wiped the tears from her face and gave Laura a beseeching look. "You would do anything...risk everything to get him back, wouldn't you?"

"Don't even go there, Julia. You have no idea what I feel

for Taylith!"

Her affection for Taylith was not something she wanted to contemplate right then. Her sister was right. She would do everything in her power to keep from losing him, especially to Zohmes and Odoxon.

From the moment she had laid eyes on the dragon at Brenn and Ciara's betrothal party, she was fascinated by him, drawn to him in ways she had never expected. Much taller than the men from Earth, he made her feel small and delicate, even though she stood five feet and nine inches. An image of him flitted through her mind. Tiny shimmering scales dotted his forehead and temples, traveling down the side of his handsome face to his neck, shoulders, and chest. Long, golden-blond hair brushed past his shoulders, and his eyes were the sparkling sapphire blue of his dragon, the pupils sometimes flashing to slits in an intriguing way when she dared to spark his anger. At first, she had made it a point to rile him whenever she could. Then on an evening her nightmares had kept her from sleep, he had taken her in his arms and held her while she purged herself of the terror of her captivity. With his help, she had learned to combat the demons that tormented her.

Julia raised a delicate brow. "Keep telling yourself that, little sister. I love John, and now that he is back, I'm not going to let him go."

Laura paced in front of the bed and glared at her sister. "John is gone, Julia. He isn't going to come back."

She knew her sister hadn't been seeing things. The man Julia had called John was Odoxon. She could see right through the illusion. When he'd tried to snatch Taylith's soul shard from her neck, a powerful force had burst from the pendant and slammed Odoxon into the wall across the room. Damn, was the bastard pissed. He had stormed out of the room, promising to flay Taylith's skin from his body, piece by piece. It would be a cold day in hell before she would ever give up his soul shard no matter what they threatened. The alternative would be much worse, and she would not lose her best friend to the two crazies. *Best friend? Who was she kidding?* He was so much more than that, but fear of being hurt again held her feelings at bay.

Visions of Taylith chained to a wall slammed into her brain. Bruises covered his face and blood poured from wounds flayed down to the bone. A reptile-like creature was chewing away his flesh. Her breath came in short pants as terror gripped her. It was a lie. It had to be. She had just spoken to him, and he was on the way with the others to break them out of this hellhole. God, she needed to hear his voice, had to know that he was fine. She tried sending her thoughts to him as he had told her the day before. *Taylith? Can you hear me?*

The sound of the lock turning in the door broke her concentration. Zohmes and Odoxon did not need to use a key, but their minions did. She stiffened. Grabbing a candlestick to use as a weapon, she turned, ready to face whatever came into the room.

"Laura!" Taylith rushed into the room and pulled her into his arms.

She dropped the candlestick and leaned into his embrace, relief pouring through her, then gazed up into those sapphire eyes and caressed his cheek. "I knew you had to be okay, that what I had just seen in my mind was a lie." She hugged him for a few moments longer, then turned to face the team. "Thank God you are all here! Julia, come on! We need to leave."

Ciara scanned the room, then looked at Julia. "Julia, where is Niqine?"

Julia pushed herself to the edge of the bed and stood, pointing to a door on the other side of the room. "In the adjoining room. They won't let me go in there."

Taylith handed Ciara the key. Like the other doors, it fit perfectly. As soon as the door opened, Niqine rushed into the room.

"I knew rescue was not far away," she said in her sweet, tinkling voice.

Julia walked toward the team, confusion clouding her features. "I don't know why you went to all this trouble. John came to get me and brought me here. I'm fine. I'm glad Laura is with me now, but she doesn't want to stay. I don't know why. Look at this place. It's beautiful!"

Ciara and Astiana each took one of Julia's hands in theirs and chanted softly. For a moment, Julia looked dazed. Laura rushed to her sister as Julia stumbled back, then looked around the room with a bewildered expression, shaking her head wildly.

"This isn't real. Is it?"

Laura placed her arm around Julia's waist to steady her. "Yes, it's very real. Zohmes and Odoxon created the illusion that you were in a glamorous room. And Odoxon made himself appear as John."

"But, Laura, it *is* John. Completely. He didn't die."

Laura heaved a sigh. "John died, Julia. Remember? Now we can't stand here and argue. We need to leave before the two bastards discover—"

She'd no sooner spoken when a man came into the room. The sight of him caused her heart to skip a beat. Julia was right. He looked exactly like John. When he spoke, he sounded just the same.

"Well, well. Our illustrious captain and her buddies paying us an unexpected visit. Julia, sweetheart, come here."

Laura held on to her sister's waist with all her might. Julia struggled, but there was no way she'd let her go.

Cewrick raised his staff and pointed it at the illusion. Green and yellow bolts of lightning shot toward the man. Within seconds, the illusion faded, and the old sorcerer stood before them, his staff in his hand, pointing it, ready to attack.

Julia screamed. "John! John! Come back! What the hell have you done with him?"

Laura tried to calm her. "Julia, you're seeing the real person. I told you it wasn't John, that they made you think he was."

Julia sobbed and leaned against Laura. "He kissed me. Several times! Everything was the same as before."

"Everything *seemed* the same. Just like this room *seemed* luxurious to you. I'm sorry, sweetie, but your John is gone, and we need to get out of here."

Zohmes suddenly appeared, his essence of pure, unadulterated hatred surrounding them. Flaming eyes gazed at the group from his hideous face. His body glowed. A loud roar came from his lips and he began to charge, but Cewrick stopped him.

"Stand together!" Cewrick shouted while holding the two figures at bay with Icaras, Astiana, Biryn, and Ciara's help. Their hands were linked. They murmured a soft chant that built into a roaring crescendo.

Laura held an almost fainting Julia tightly in her arms. Just before their transport began, a white-clad figure rushed out of the room Niqine had occupied and joined them. She didn't have time to react or think.

Cewrick shouted, "Now!"

A loud buzzing sound hurt her ears, a twirling sensation, then a feeling as if she were sucked into a vacuum cleaner.

CHAPTER NINE

The dragons landed safely within the perimeter of the shield. The embers of the fire still glowed. Biryn, Brenn, Aldis, Erica, and Laro rushed to the stranger that had stepped into their circle just before their transport.

"Who are you?" Brenn demanded.

Taylith looked at the young man. He was dressed in a white spacesuit with an emblem embroidered on the left shoulder depicting a circle of two lions and a dragon. He had long, flaming red hair that hung in waves to his shoulders, very blue eyes, and a kind face. He was young, maybe in his early twenties. The man strongly reminded Taylith of Zohmes. The man's gaze was riveted on Julia. He hesitated, then took a step toward her. "Mother? But how…"

Taylith drew his sword and stepped in front of Julia and Laura while Brenn and Aldis grabbed the stranger and held him back.

The man struggled, trying to get to Julia. "Let me go! She's my mother!"

"What are you talking about! Who the hell are you!" Julia's voice trembled.

Confusion clouded the man's face. "Mom! Don't you know who I am? It's me, Jonathan!"

"What in the hell are you talking about! My sister doesn't have any children. Especially one your age," Laura said in a heated tone, then softer, "Julia, honey, you need to calm down. It's not good for the baby."

Jonathan stopped struggling against Brenn and Aldis' hold. "Aunt Laura, please! Is she going to be okay?"

"Keep him back. If you need to, put a binding spell on him." Taylith lowered his sword and turned to Julia and Laura. Julia's face was as white as a sheet, her body trembled, and her breath came in gasps between sobs. "Ciara, can you help her?"

Ciara slipped beside them and brushed her fingers across Julia's forehead. Julia calmed quickly but leaned against Laura for support. "She needs to rest. This whole ordeal has been a shock."

"I have placed a containment field around Jonathan until we learn more. This doesn't feel like an illusion, but I don't want to take any chances." Cewrick chanted briefly. Red glowing rings appeared around the young man.

Satisfied that Jonathan would cause Julia no further distress, Taylith fetched three blankets to drape around Niqine, Zandria, and Julia, who wore nothing but a thin white gown.

"Thank you, Taylith." Laura took the blanket from his hand and draped it around Julia's shoulders. "I brought extra clothing and a skin suit for Julia but not for Niqine. Julia, come with me to change. It's freezing." She ushered her sister to her tent.

"I brought an extra skin suit. It will be a bit big for Niqine, but it will keep her warm. Thankfully, she wore winter clothing to go to the market. Come, Niqine, you need to change into the suit." Ciara held the little woman's hand as if she were leading a child.

Of course none of them had known they would be rescuing Zandria, and the blanket would do little to keep her warm. Taylith shrugged his coat off and handed it to the young woman. "This should keep you much warmer than the blanket."

"Thank you." She smiled gratefully and slipped it around her shoulders.

"Izarus' shield is still in place around the camp, but we cannot stay here," Biryn said. "We need to return to the palace."

Taylith stood and pointed at Ciara's backpack where it lay near the fire. "Not until I return the shards. I am sure they belong to the ten black dragons at Blood Lagoon. We have lost too many and I will not ignore their plight. I am going to free them."

Ivran had thrown more wood on the embers. It ignited and soon began to warm them. Ciara returned with Niqine, the little woman now visibly warmer. They joined the others by the fire.

"I heard your last words, Taylith. I will not allow them to be bound at Blood Lagoon any longer either. We must go forthwith. Rania will assist us in returning the shards to the black dragons." Ciara held her hands closer to the flames.

"Go now. We need to leave this place," Biryn told them.

Taylith grabbed Ciara's pack containing the urn. "There is no need for you to wait for us. Ciara and I can fly back to the palace."

"No. We came as a team and we shall return as a team. Izarus' shield will keep us safe," Biryn said stubbornly.

Ciara shrugged. "As you wish. Come, Taylith."

They left the campsite and hurried to the open space to shift into their dragons.

The urn easily fit in the grasp of Ciara's front claw. The

shards within it allowed them to approach the lagoon. Like before, ten black dragons circled above the red water. Taylith and Ciara landed and changed into their humans. Taking the lid off the urn, Ciara spread the shards on the red sand.

Rania appeared. "Are you ready?"

The three joined hands while Rania cast her spell over the soul shards. Just like in Cewrick's castle, they faded and disappeared.

Almost instantly, the black dragons changed into their jeweled beauty. The dragons circled above them for a few moments before flying away. Two of them, a red dragon and a larger golden dragon, descended and landed near them.

Ciara grasped his arm. "Is that…"

Taylith's heart pounded as the dragons changed into their humans. Overwhelmed with emotion, he nodded. "I thought my father and mother had been killed."

Copera rushed to embrace them, her blonde hair flying behind her as she ran. Jelano clasped his son, Ciara, and his mate in his arms. The four stood huddled together, tears unashamedly soaking their faces.

When Taylith finally stepped out of the embrace, the Blood Lagoon was no more. It had returned to its former beauty, very much resembling the Clyss.

Jelano clapped Taylith on the shoulder. "Son, thank you and Ciara for coming to our aid, and thanks to the goddess Rania."

"The gods had answered my prayers when I had seen you and Ciara escape Cewrick just before he took us." Copera's eyes shimmered with tears.

Ciara brushed her hair from her eyes, her face contorted in pain. "Taylith did not escape. He sacrificed his freedom to ensure I evaded capture."

Taylith hated the idea that his parents had been bound to

the Blood Lagoon. If not for the vision the god I Am had given him, his mother and father would still be trapped. "After the curse was broken, you didn't return. I thought you both had been killed."

Copera gasped. "The curse is broken? But how?"

"My brother! Ciara, your parents, are they safe?" Jelano's voice cracked with emotion.

Ciara smiled. "My parents are at the Tideless Abyss, as are the rest of our people. I am glad to see you both alive and I know Father and Mother will be, too."

Taylith gazed at his parents. He had much to be thankful for, but the quest to defeat Zohmes was far from over. "Ciara and her lifemate, Brenn, and Cewrick's son, Icaras, defeated Cewrick and broke the curse. We must now defeat Zohmes and Odoxon. Zohmes wishes to rule Ierilia."

Ciara placed her hand on his arm, a troubled expression in her eyes. "We must continue this discussion later. Taylith and I must hurry back to the team and return to the palace. It is not safe for the king to tarry near the Dreaded Peaks."

Jelano put his arm around Copera. "We will join the others at the Tideless Abyss. I long to reunite with my brother, and there is much work to be done if we are to protect the king."

Taylith embraced his parents again with the promise they would soon get together. He and Ciara called out their dragons and flew swiftly back to the camp. By the time they had returned, the team had packed up already and were waiting by the hovercraft. Zandria was still with them, now dressed in one of Erica's battlesuits.

Brenn finished dousing the fire. "Icaras and Cewrick offered to return Zandria to her village, but she is afraid to go back. She can come with us for a while. I have promised we will contact her family that she is safe and in Cront. Her mother lives in the forest near Cidus' castle. I will contact

Evior on his tablet."

"What do we do about Cidus and Evior? We cannot continue to allow the people of this realm to be used as sacrifices." The idea that Cidus had been capturing and using his people as tools to further Zohmes' quest for power made him ache to rain fire upon the man.

Biryn gave Taylith a pained look. "We can do nothing at this point. We have no proof of Cidus' involvement yet. Evior has expressed the wish to join my army, but he is too afraid of his father for now."

Laura stepped up beside him and caressed his arm. "Brenn told me you went back to the Blood Lagoon. Were you and Ciara able to free the others?"

Gods, she took his breath away, even with the smudge of dirt that darkened her right cheek. He reached up to wipe it off, needing the feel of her skin beneath his fingertips. "Yes, Rania assisted us to return their shards. My parents were with them. They are safely on their way back home."

She stood on her tiptoes and kissed him on the cheek. "I am so glad to hear they are alive and okay."

Julia joined them, edging away from the young man that claimed to be her son. Her face was pale, her eyes trained on Jonathan. Laura turned her attention to Julia and led her aboard the hovercraft.

Taylith took a seat beside Laura and strapped himself in. Julia sat on the other side of her. She appeared calm for the moment, but with their new passenger, that could change quickly.

Cewrick directed Jonathan to a seat away from them. Once Jonathan was secured, he took the seat beside him. "He is still within my containment spell."

Jonathan turned to Biryn. "I hope, when we arrive at your palace, I can convince you of the truth."

"We shall see," Biryn said.

It was dinnertime when they arrived at the palace. Before joining Biryn and Cylena in the king's quarters, they all went to their rooms to bathe and change clothes. A servant took Niqine and Zandria to a guest room, and Cewrick took Jonathan along to his room.

Taylith wanted nothing more than to be alone with Laura, they still had so much to discuss, but she had gone with Julia to her room. And that was good because Julia should not be alone that night. He sighed. Zohmes would stop at nothing to get Julia back into his clutches. Ciara had told them that Rania would keep the young woman safe, but there was still this night to get through. He quickly bathed, changed into clean clothes, and hurried to Biryn's quarters.

When he entered the dining room, he was surprised that Jonathan was sitting at the table. The man had sounded crazy when they were at the campsite. Everyone else was already there as well, except Laura and Julia.

He toyed with his food, worry about the girls clouding his mind. Through the bond they shared, he could feel the pain riding Laura, knew how worried she was for her sister and the baby, even though her first reaction had been to have her sister terminate the pregnancy. Finally, they came in. Julia had obviously been crying and Laura did not look happy.

"Sorry we're late," Laura apologized as they sat.

Taylith suspected that Julia still was not convinced that John was not real and that they had yanked her away from the man she loved.

"Julia, can I talk to you privately for a few minutes?" Ciara did not wait for an answer. Instead she held her hand out to Julia.

It was good that Ciara had drawn Julia into Biryn's

bedroom. Taylith knew she could explain everything better than anyone and would keep Julia calm. He looked at Laura toying with her food, throwing concerned glances at the bedroom door. "She will be fine after Ciara talks to her," he reassured her.

She tried to smile but worry still radiated from her. "I sure hope so. I couldn't get it through her head that it wasn't John she had been with in that temple. But if anyone can convince her, it's Ciara."

"Cewrick, how is Hirsuta?" Biryn asked.

"She is recovering well. Thank you for asking. It will not be long before Catrice will allow her out of bed."

"I can hardly wait." Cylena stroked Biryn's arm for a moment, obviously happy to have him home again.

Ciara and Julia returned to the table. Taylith noticed Julia looked much calmer now and seemed at peace, except when she glanced at Jonathan. Her expression became troubled again.

Ciara sat and nibbled at her food before she began to speak. "I did not explain everything to Julia. I wanted to wait until you can all hear what Rania has disclosed to me."

"When did you communicate with Rania?" Taylith asked.

"During our flight home. You all know that Rania intended to spirit Julia and her unborn baby away so that she would be safe from Zohmes and Odoxon. That plan changed. The gods and goddesses brought Jonathan to us from the future. He is truly Julia's son."

"It can't be true! I am carrying John's baby!" Julia jumped up from her chair.

"Sit down, Julia. I am not finished. If Rania would have put the original plan into action, you would have disappeared from everyone, from Laura. Your baby would be born, and you would both have been safe, but it could be many years before we defeat Zohmes and the sorcerer. This way, you are still with your sister and your people. But you are no longer carrying the baby. Jonathan is that baby, and he is Zohmes' son, not John's."

"Impossible!" Julia jumped up again, placing her hands on her belly as if protecting the unborn infant.

"Nothing is impossible for the gods and goddesses. Remember, Zohmes is a god. He desired Julia for himself. While John was asleep, Zohmes disguised himself as John and was familiar with Julia. That is when she conceived. Cewrick, you can remove Jonathan's restraints. He speaks the truth."

"I don't believe any of it, especially that I'm carrying Satan's baby. I want to see Catrice!" Julia shouted.

Biryn tapped his plate with his fork. "Calm down, Julia. Brenn, contact Catrice and see if she can see Julia?"

Taylith was concerned about Julia's pale face, her troubled eyes. This was a huge shock for her. "Jonathan, how old are you?"

"I'm twenty-four. I am as shocked by all this as my mother."

"Can you tell us what exactly happened? What do you remember?" Biryn asked.

"I was getting ready to go on a space mission. The next I knew I was in that room and saw all of you standing in a group and the light whirling around you."

Biryn's face lit and he smiled. "You can tell us what happens in the next twenty-four years. Do we defeat Zohmes and Odoxon?"

Taylith waited for Jonathan's answer with anticipation. But it was not what Biryn had hoped.

"Strangely, I don't remember anything. I recognized Julia as my mother, whom I love dearly, but I can't remember growing up."

Astiana interjected. "No. We are not allowed to know. You and your mother will need to make new memories. It will be very difficult for both of you, especially for Julia, as she will have no memory of birthing you, holding you in her arms, or raising you."

"Catrice will see Julia now. Laura, do you want to take her to the clinic?" Brenn asked.

Taylith watched Laura lead a distraught Julia out of the king's quarters. He wished he could be with them, be there for Laura. Her heart had to be breaking for her sister.

"It's like my life before this has been erased," Jonathan complained. "And now you're telling me that the god Zohmes is really my father and not John? I find that hard to believe. I don't have any godly powers."

Astiana set her fork on her plate. "Oh, but you do. After all has settled and you begin your life anew, we will take you to the Clyss. As Zohmes' son, you have inherited his powers and more. You will be more powerful."

"If I wasn't stunned before, now my mind is blown." Jonathan ran his fingers through his hair.

"You sure talk like your mother and Laura," Taylith commented.

"I recognized Aunt Laura, too. Strange, I love both of them. I remember that. But I can't recall anything else. Will it always stay that way? Do I just continue living here now?"

"Do not feel bad, Jonathan. I will tell you my story one day. I had just as much catching up to do." Icaras grinned at the young man.

Laura and Julia returned from their visit to the infirmary. They sat at the table, but Julia was very quiet. Taylith noticed her furtively glancing at Jonathan from beneath her lashes.

"Catrice confirmed it. Julia is not pregnant anymore. She also ran a DNA test. Jonathan did not notice, but I plucked a hair from his head. The test showed that John is not the father, but Julia is his mother." Laura placed an arm around her sister's shoulders.

Julia pushed Laura's arm away. "But how? John is dead. She needs his tissue or blood."

"Honey, there were blood samples from all of us on the ship, and they took samples after examining us when we were rescued. Yes, they had John's blood," Laura patiently explained, "And I gave her Jonathan's hair."

"So Jonathan is my son? For real? I have a grown-up son that I don't remember giving birth to or raising?"

"Yes, he is," Ciara told her.

"Zohmes' son? My child is Satan's son? I can't believe it!" Julia became agitated again.

"Satan?" Jonathan queried.

"That is where your memory fails you. I am sure your mother taught you all this while raising you. On Earth, people worship one God. There was a fallen angel, Lucifer, the devil, or Satan, as people called him. He was bad, like Zohmes. At least, that is how Erica explained it. Erica? Maybe you can help out here?" Laro said.

Erica snickered. "You explained it very well. But just because Zohmes is a badass god, it doesn't mean Jonathan is evil. Looking at him, Julia did a damn good job raising him."

Ivran stood and looked at them all. "This has been quite the adventure. I would like to go home to my family now, if that is okay?"

They all decided it was time to rest for the night. Taylith watched Laura take off with Julia. His heart ached for her but longed for her at the same time. Right now, he could not reach out to her. Her sister's needs came first.

CHAPTER TEN

Taylith shifted restlessly in his bed. He dared not close his eyes to sleep. Visions of his slavery to Cewrick bombarded his mind, playing over and over, plaguing him with the atrocities he had been forced into performing for the twisted bastard. The sorcerer was lucky that when he was on Garissa Island, he had felt the truth, *knew* that Zohmes had possessed him. If it were not for that knowledge, Taylith would have ripped the man apart, piece by bloody piece.

He shoved his feet to the floor and stood, making his way to the balcony. He did not care how cold it was outside. He needed some fresh air. He opened the door and stepped out onto the veranda. Snow fell heavily from the sky, blanketing the grounds in pristine white. Bracing his hands on the railing of the balcony, he stared beyond the city to the wooded hillsides and mountain peaks rising in the distance. For now, the realm was peaceful, but war loomed ahead. Their planet would be peaceful no more. Plans had been made, events set in motion. The vision he had been given was only the tip of the iceberg.

Arms slid around his waist, and a warm body pressed against his back. "Taylith, you need to come inside! You are a block of ice!"

He closed his eyes for a moment and savored the heat of her embrace, then turned and studied her face. Worry flashed in those beautiful green eyes as she met his gaze. "Laura, why are you here? Is your sister well?"

She released her hold, then grabbed him by the arm, trying to force him inside. "Julia is fine, but you aren't. Come on, we need to get you warm."

He had not felt the cold until she had freed him from her embrace. He allowed her to lead him back into the room, then pulled the door closed behind them. He turned to face Laura. Her hand rested on her hip and she tapped her foot on the floor. Anger replaced the worry in her eyes. To his satisfaction, she still wore his soul shard around her neck.

She turned, grabbed a blanket from his bed, and threw it at him. "What in the hell were you doing out there in the freezing cold half-dressed? Do you want to get sick?"

He draped the blanket around his shoulders and reached for her hand. Unlike the last time he had faced her anger, she allowed him to take it. "I am well, Laura. There is nothing to worry about."

She stepped into his arms and gave him a pointed look. "Then why were you out in the snow brooding?"

Not wanting to answer her question, he evaded the subject. He had no wish to share the memories that tainted his soul. "You never answered me. What brought you to my room?"

"It was something Julia said to me before she fell asleep. I needed my best friend." She sighed and sat down on the edge of his bed and motioned for him to sit beside her. When he joined her, she leaned against him and kissed his shoulder.

He was beginning to resign himself to being nothing more than her friend. She referred to him as such so often, but her actions spoke a different story. He shifted on the bed to lean his back against the pillows, pulling her with him. "What did your sister tell you?"

"She told me that if I care for someone that I shouldn't let him slip away and that I was a dumbass for letting what Ryan did to me stop me from pursuing happiness." She snuggled up to him and rested her head on his shoulder. "I need to ask you something and I need you to tell me the truth."

He hugged her close and kissed the top of her head. He knew he deserved that barb after he had withheld who he was from her. He had spent many evenings with her when they were both too consumed by the demons that rode them to sleep. She had confided in him, told him what had happened during her captivity, the torture, her brush with death. "No more secrets."

She looked up at him and nodded. "No more secrets… You didn't give me your soul shard because you were forced to, did you? Because it was written in the book of knowledge?"

He tilted her chin and kissed her gently, then gazed down at her beautiful face. "I gave you my soul shard because I love you, Laura. I would have given it to you even if you were not my lifemate."

Her eyes widened in surprise. She quickly tamped it down, a determined look filling her gaze. "How do you know for sure that we are lifemates?"

Taylith knew what he was about to do would open a floodgate between them. Her fear had stifled their bond, but the only way to explain how he knew they were lifemates was to show her. There would be no more secrets between them. Even the darkness of his past could not be shut away. He picked up the pendant and placed it in her hand. The shard started to glow as soon as it touched her palm. He closed her fingers around it and held her hand in his. "Close your eyes and just feel."

The glow from his soul shard enveloped them in its

warmth. He heard her gasp as their connection flared to life, the shackles placed upon it by them both burned away. A dam had burst between them, and the feelings she had kept safely hidden away set his soul on fire. He gently pried her fingers from the shard and let it fall to her chest, their connection still a living breathing thing. The light that surrounded them dissipated and she slowly opened her eyes.

"Taylith..."

A tear slid down her cheek. He carefully wiped it away, hating the idea that he had upset her once again. He clenched his jaw. "I am sorry. I should not have done that."

"No, you will not be sorry for giving me the truth." She wrapped her arms around his neck and kissed him, then gave him a heated look "Your soul isn't tainted by the past, Taylith, no matter how you may feel about it, and I won't allow you to suffer the pain alone."

"I do not have full memory of my life as a black dragon, but knowing what we all did, the horrors that I know I inflicted on people, eats at me."

"But you were under Cewrick's spell. Eh...I should say Zohmes. Can't Ciara help you with this?"

"No, her powers are limited to healing the body, not what plagues the mind, and before you ask, I will not allow her to remove the memories of it. The sacrifices others have made to free Ierilia of evil should never be forgotten."

Laura pulled back from him suddenly and sat on her knees. She pulled her strange little Earth nightgown off over her head and threw it aside, then removed the blanket from his shoulders. When she pressed her breasts against him, the fire within ignited in full force.

"Taylith, I am falling in love with you. I've been fighting against my feelings, because of the past, but Julia gave me wise counsel. If I have a chance at happiness, I must grab it with both hands. And I'm doing so now."

He gazed into her eyes, saw how earnest she was. Surely this was a dream? No, it was no dream that her fingers skated down his chest, to his abdomen, searing his skin as they traveled to the dip below the waist of his pants. She loosened the tie and, swiftly stripping him of them, stroked his cock from tip to base. Gods, she took his breath away. His body was on fire for her, her boldness inflaming the desire coursing through his veins. He groaned as she bent and took the head into her mouth, teasing the tip with her tongue. She sucked while her fingers of one hand moved the skin back and forth, her other hand playing with his sack. His balls were so taut, he thought they would burst. If she did not stop, he would come. Reaching down, he pulled her up until she lay on top of him.

"Slow down..." He took a deep breath to steady his pounding heart, to still the fire for now. She took his face between her hands, then with a fingertip, stroked his forehead, his nose, his lips, until she claimed his mouth in an unending kiss. Their tongues explored. When she sucked his tongue deep into her mouth, he embraced her tightly and swiveled her onto her back.

Gazing down at her, for a moment he admired her firm breasts, her nipples poking out from a dark aureole. He ached to touch...to taste...to devour every inch of her soft alabaster skin. He traced his fingers along the underside of her breast, around her aureole, then took it in his hand. He bent to sample the delectable treat before him, her body arching to meet the assault of his teeth and tongue. A soft sigh escaped her when he continued his onslaught, caressing her neglected breast and tweaking the nipple with his fingers.

She moaned beneath his caresses. Her hips bucked up against him, rubbing her belly against his cock. He nipped her nipple one more time, then rained little kisses all the way down to her bellybutton. He stopped for a moment, surprised by the gold ring he found there. But only for a few seconds. The flare of her hips and the soft tuft of blonde hair at the apex of her thighs was much more intriguing. Her body trembling, she parted her legs for him. He sat on his knees and admired the heaven that awaited him. Pink folds, her clit pulsing invitingly, begging to be sucked. He took the little nub into his mouth and sucked hard while his fingers sought her entrance.

Her nectar flowed freely, soaking his fingers. He entered one, then two, and moved them deep within her. To his surprise, he encountered a barrier. She was a virgin? He stopped and looked at her. "Laura, are you sure? You have never…"

"No, not completely. Please, Taylith? I want this…I want you and if I am your lifemate, I am yours to take." Her voice was husky, her lips parted, her eyes sparkling with desire.

"We can wait until we are officially joined."

"Like bloody hell. This needs to happen. Tonight."

Gods, he ached for her, needed to sink his aching cock deep within her lush folds. Her words only incited the hunger that drove him. Not wanting to hurt her, he tempered his passion, continuing his exploration until her body trembled and her cries of ecstasy filled the air.

He shifted upward, his lips skimming her abdomen, her breasts, then her mouth. He grasped his cock and placed the tip against the slick wetness of her core. Suddenly, she bucked up, causing him to gain entry. He heard her gasp as he filled her, stretching the walls. He leaned forward, kneading her breasts as he edged in slowly until the barrier stopped him. Taking her into his arms, he claimed her lips while he thrust and broke through.

94

Her legs clamped around him, urging him to keep moving.

"Take me, baby. Please, take me," he heard her beg through the pounding of his heart in his ears.

He did. He could no longer stop himself. She met him stroke for stroke until she broke free of his lips and flung her head wildly from side to side.

"I'm coming!"

Her body shuddered, and he allowed his own release to take control. He kissed her tenderly, then whispered against her lips, "I love you, Laura."

Spent, they lay quietly for a little while until Taylith rolled away. "I have some chairi wine. Would you like some?"

"Please?" She took the glass he handed her, then nestled beside him. "Taylith, I love you, too. Ciara said it was different with dragons because of the soul shard. Does this mean we are now one?"

"Not until the joining, sweetness." He lifted the pendant containing his shard from between her breasts. "The gods and goddesses will complete our bond if you so choose. You will no longer need to wear my soul shard."

"Of course I *choose* to, Taylith." She covered his hand with hers. "Let's make that soon? When the priests captured me, Odoxon tried to rip the pendant from my neck. A magical force kept him from taking it, but I am afraid he will try again. I don't want to lose you."

He dropped the pendant and twined his fingers with hers. "We need to first deal with the issues encountered during this mission. Julia is going to need you. Suddenly having a grown son that she does not remember birthing, it is a lot to handle."

Laura sighed. "I know. I can hardly believe it myself. I have a grown nephew. And to top it all, he's Satan's son."

"Except for his fiery hair and piercing eyes, it does not appear he has inherited Zohmes' personality and evil ways."

"It's going to take Julia a few months to accept it all and for them to get to know each other. If only Jonathan could tell us of the twenty-four years he has already lived."

Taylith took the empty wineglasses and set them on the bedside table, then nestled Laura against his chest. "Did I imagine it, or did you call me baby?"

She giggled. "It's often used on Earth as an endearment."

The sound of her laughter was a balm to his soul. He had made it a point to make her smile when he had first moved to Brenn's estate.

He twisted a lock of her silky blonde hair around his finger. "You are so beautiful."

"Hey, you aren't half-bad yourself." She playfully pinched his nipples.

"Ouch. If you start that, you will get me all hot again." Shifting his body over hers, he caged her beneath him, then leaned down and nipped her chin.

"Go for it, baby!"

Taylith frowned before he kissed her long and hard. He would need to talk to her about this *baby* word. He was hardly an infant.

CHAPTER ELEVEN

Taylith woke to the feel of Laura nestled tightly against him. Her head rested on his shoulder, and her leg was draped across his abdomen. She was still sleeping soundly. He carefully disengaged himself from her and tenderly caressed her cheek, hating that he would have to wake her. He glanced at the windows. It had stopped snowing and the suns were already shining brightly into his room. If they did not get moving, they would be late.

"Laura, wake up. We are supposed to meet in the king's chambers for breakfast."

She sleepily rubbed her eyes. "Hell, we were up nearly all night. All I want to do is sleep. It's your fault."

He could not help but smile. Her desire for him was as ravenous as his hunger for her. They had spent most of the night discovering just how insatiable they both were. "You need to go and check on Julia."

She pulled him down and kissed him. "We're a couple now? We're engaged?"

"If you mean we are betrothed, yes… That is if you wish to be?"

She grinned at him, her face lit with happiness. "Yes, I wish to be. I want to announce it so badly. But because of Julia, maybe we should wait?"

"Yes, I agree. But the team will notice anyway that things have changed between us."

Laura bathed first and, after a quick kiss, hurried to join her sister. Taylith silently thanked the gods and goddesses. His wish had come true that night. He hurried to bathe and get dressed. Biryn did not like to be kept waiting.

When he joined the team at the breakfast table, he was surprised to see Hirsuta sitting by Cewrick's side. The transformation was remarkable. She had recuperated fast. Her hair was now washed and cut, and she was dressed in a stylish dress. He could see from who Cylena had inherited her beauty and Icaras his handsome face.

"Good morning, everyone," he greeted. "Hirsuta, I am so happy to see you have recovered well from your ordeal."

Cewrick introduced him. "This is Taylith. He is one of the team and Ciara's cousin."

"You must be Jelano's son. I was quite close to Brokig and Jelano, the dragon twins."

"Yes, Jelano is my father," Taylith told her.

"And I learned that you just rescued your father and mother from the Blood Lagoon. You must be overjoyed. Did they return to the Storming Enclave?"

Taylith gave her a confused look. "Yes, we thought they had perished during the curse, but I have never heard of the Storming Enclave. My parents have returned to our home, the Tideless Abyss."

Laura walked in with Julia before Hirsuta could answer. She took the seat beside him, gave him a bright smile, then caressed his leg. Julia sat next to Astiana. More introductions were made. Then the servants began to bring in breakfast.

He turned to Hirsuta, his curiosity piqued. "What is the Storming Enclave?" Before the curse he and Ciara would take wing and explore the realms. He had never seen nor heard of the place.

"The Storming Enclave is the sister city of the Tideless Abyss. How could you not know of it? Jelano was its ruler."

"Both Taylith and I were born and grew up at the Tideless Abyss. There is no other city that I know of," Ciara stated.

Cewrick gasped, drawing Taylith's attention. The man's back was ramrod straight, an agitated look crossing his face.

"It is not Niqine's disappearance that has caused the disease afflicting the vegetation in the Xynnar Valley and the unstableness of the Koriam crystals." Cewrick looked at both Taylith and Ciara. "Your fathers, they are twins, correct?"

Taylith frowned. "What does that have to do with dying plants in Xynnar and a city we have never heard of?"

Ciara shrugged. "Yes, they are identical. If you did not know them well, you would not be able to tell them apart."

"If they are twins, why didn't Taylith inherit all of his father's magick, like Ciara inherited Brokig's?" Icaras commented.

Taylith shot Icaras an annoyed look. Both he and Ciara had trained extensively to use magick. The gods only knew why his father had forced him into the training. He could manage some small things, like the flowers he had given to Brenn to help Laura and Mark in the forbidden forest. The powers given to the team at the Clyss before they rescued Cylena did not work for him. Ciara and her father were the true sorcerers of their family. "My father is not a sorcerer, Icaras."

Hirsuta brushed her hair out of her pale face. "Of course he is, Taylith. He was just as powerful as his brother. And he will be again."

Cewrick tapped his fingers on the table to get their attention. "During Zohmes' first attempt to enslave the dragons, he used our combined powers to breach the

Storming Enclave. He did not succeed in capturing the dragons then, but he did manage to corrupt the land and bind Jelano's power, forcing him to move his people to the Tideless Abyss. That all happened long before Ciara and Taylith were born. The corruption must be lifted from the land, and the jeweled dragons must return to the Storming Enclave."

Taylith was beginning to think the whole lot of them had lost their minds. *Do you think our fathers would have hidden something like this from us?* Ciara's question interrupted his thoughts.

He and Ciara had barely come of age when the dragons were cursed. Anything could have happened during the centuries before they were born. *I do not know, but you must admit we were very reckless when we were young. We would have gone looking for it. If our fathers kept it from us, they did it for our own safety.*

"How will this help the problem in the Xynnar Valley?" Brenn inquired.

"Storming Enclave's floating island was above Xynnar Valley, though still connected to the Tideless Abyss. When Zohmes placed the curse on the jeweled dragons, the gods and goddesses sent Niqine's handmaidens to the Tideless Abyss and placed a strong protection spell around it. But they could not protect Storming Enclave. Zohmes had already claimed and cursed it. I suspect they placed something on the island or in its city and they have recently activated it, causing the curse on the crops, hothouses, and vegetation around Xynnar."

"But Niqine's village within the crater is intact and verdant." Icaras frowned, a bewildered expression on his face.

"The gods and goddesses also immediately placed a spell on Niqine's village and the crater, protecting it."

"So in order to save our crops and vegetation, we need to travel to this unheard of place?" Ivran asked.

Cewrick nodded. "If I am correct, and Ciara can verify with Rania, yes. We will need to go to Storming Enclave."

Brenn sat back in his chair and crossed his arms. "I have never seen a floating island above Xynnar."

"Like the Tideless Abyss, it is not visible to human eyes. Or a lion's eyes," Astiana answered.

"How do we get there?" Laro inquired.

"The same way we went to the Tideless Abyss. Ciara and Taylith will need to fly us. This time we will not need permission to step onto its land," Cewrick said.

Hirsuta toyed with the food on her plate. "I will go with you."

Cylena gasped and looked at Hirsuta. "No. You are far too weak, Mother." Her voice was firm as she spoke. "I cannot go because I am carrying the heir to the throne. I need you to be by my side."

"Child, you are not ill."

Cylena laughed. "No, I am not, but you are barely recovering. There will be many missions in the future. I am sure of that."

Taylith had listened to the interaction and tried to clear his mind of all the jumbled information. "To be clear, we need to return Niqine to her village. Then we need to find Storming Enclave and find out what Zohmes concocted there to cause our vegetation, crops, and hothouse vegetables to wilt and almost die and make the crystals unstable. The question is, what are we looking for? How do we find it? How do we even locate the floating island?"

Ciara pushed her chair back and stood. "I will return shortly."

They continued picking at their breakfast, each lost in their own thoughts. Until Jonathan spoke.

"I haven't dared to say much because I am so new to all this. But can I be a part of this mission? Please?"

Julia jumped up, sending her chair almost flying. "No! I lost you once by not being allowed to continue my pregnancy, give birth to you, or raise you, and I've barely met you. I won't have you risking your life for a cause you don't know anything about."

Laura folded her napkin and looked at her sister. "Julia, it is up to the king. Actually, it is up to Rania. She will tell Ciara what we need to do and who is to go. Sit down. Calm yourself. You have many years ahead to get to know your son."

"Thank you, Aunt Laura, but I can defend myself. Mother, knowing I am that evil being's son boils my innards. I would like to be a major member of defeating him and the pain and harm he has caused. You must understand that. I might be his son, but I'm ashamed for anyone to know that. By the sounds of it, the man, or as I'm told, a god, is pure evil."

"Your language is like your mother's and Laura's. I wish you could remember your twenty-four years. But alas, I understand why you cannot. We are not allowed to know everything," Biryn told him. "You may participate in the mission, Jonathan."

Ciara returned. She sat and looked at them all. "Rania told me to listen to Cewrick. His explanation is close to correct. Zohmes has placed something on Storming Enclave that he empowered to begin the demise of our crops and vegetation. We must find it by going to the island."

Taylith finished eating his eggs. "So how do we find the island?"

"Rania, with the help of the gods and goddesses, will guide us. She warned we will encounter danger. All but Cylena, Hirsuta, and Julia must go. Julia, you will stay here at the palace for now for your safety. Jonathan, you will accompany us. You have the power to undo what your father began."

Jonathan scowled. "Last night you mentioned I had powers. I have never felt anything, and I wouldn't even know how to use magick if I had the ability."

"The Clyss. We must take you there so that your powers are activated, then help you learn to use them. There are three steps to this mission. Go to the Clyss. Return Niqine to her village. Then find Storming Enclave and stop the annihilation of our means of survival. Our storage units are depleting fast, and the farmers are in uproar."

Taylith frowned. "What are we looking for? Did Rania tell you?"

Ciara shook her head. "No. She only said we would know when we laid eyes upon it."

They left soon after they had finished breakfast. Their supplies were mostly still packed from their previous mission, so they only had to add more food and fresh waterskins and wineskins.

Taylith and Ciara landed near the Bottomless Basin in the Clyss. After their passengers had slid from their backs and stepped onto the banks of the pool, they shifted to their humans.

"It is always so beautiful here. Like we're in a different country. No snow here. Is it always like this?" Laura stepped beside him and clasped his hand.

"Yes, it is. The Clyss is sacred to the gods and is always under their protection."

Unlike many of the realms during the months of snow and frost, the Clyss was bursting with color. Lush flowers dotted the ground all the way up to the edge of the water. It was hard to believe plant life was dying on the other side of the ridge.

"So what happens now?" Jonathan stood beside Ciara, his hands shoved in his pockets.

"Now we call upon Izarus for his assistance. Come, Jonathan, you must follow us." Ciara turned to Taylith. "You, too, Taylith."

Ciara, what would be the point? The last time the gods bestowed magick, their gifts didn't work.

Ciara gave him an impatient look. *Of course it did. What do you think shielded Laura when she entered the Blood Lagoon?*

Taylith squeezed Laura's hand, then released it to follow Jonathan, Astiana, Cewrick, Icaras, and Ciara to the clearing near the waterfall. Before they could even join their hands together, the sound of thunder reverberated through the valley. The sky darkened to almost pitch-black and the wind whipped around them like a cyclone.

Suddenly, a bolt of lightning flashed above them, and the bright blade of fire struck the ground hard within the circle of their bodies. Taylith grabbed Ciara's arm to keep her from falling. They grasped hands as they looked up at the god. The light surrounding him was so bright, it hurt Taylith's eyes.

"I am who I Am, the maker of all gods and goddesses, of magick, and the creator of all that is, was, and shall be." The booming voice of I Am sounded around them and echoed throughout the Clyss.

Taylith let go of Ciara's hand to shield his eyes. A hazy mist swirled above them. Within the mist, he saw a face, but it kept changing. It was as if he was viewing images of hundreds of faces. Glowing particles rained down. A hand appeared, holding a staff so glorious, it was indescribable. Its top resembled a lion's head, but like the faces, it kept changing, from lion to dragon, to a jewel, to a skull, to a reptile. It rotated so fast Taylith could hardly keep up with its many facets. It emitted a radiant glow that changed colors.

"My daughter, Rania, has called upon me to ask for my assistance. My anger at Zohmes surpasses all else, so I have seen fit to grant her request."

The god pinned Taylith with a penetrating stare, the faces everchanging. He recognized many that had lost their lives during Cewrick's reign, the souls he had extinguished during his enslavement. Pain ripped through him, driving him to his knees. Tendrils of immense power weaved their way through his body until they gripped his very essence, his soul bared to the god before him. And still the faces changed, this time to ones he had protected, those he loved, and the woman he cherished above all others. As quickly as the power had taken hold, it released him. Taking a deep, shuddering breath, he staggered to his feet.

"Taylith, you question the powers I bestowed upon you. They were restored to you in full force before your mission to Yanata. You must believe in the brightness of your soul. I would not have chosen you as the vessel of my prophesies if your soul had been stained by evil. Cast your doubts aside and embrace your gifts."

Taylith was relieved when I Am turned his attention to Jonathan. Another bolt of lightning jolted from above, directly at Jonathan. Taylith watched him stumble, almost fall to the ground, but he caught himself.

"Jonathan. Child, you are the son of a human mother from another planet, and Zohmes. You have inherited your father's powers, but they must be activated. I have done so. I will warn you. Because of Zohmes' iniquities, his falling from grace, he has angered me and all the gods and goddesses. We will watch you. Use your powers with great care and wisdom. Should you falter, fail, you will suffer the same inevitable fate as Zohmes. May the goodness of your mother prevail. You both must now enter the basin. I have spoken."

The clouds dissipated, and the sky cleared. The suns now shone brightly above them.

Taylith was still shaken from I Am's perusal of him. "The bottomless basin? Is that why my powers did not activate completely?"

Ciara punched his arm, an exasperated look in her eyes. "Yes, I believe so." *How could you believe that your soul is tainted?* She pushed him toward the pool.

You would believe the same if it had been you Cewrick enslaved.

Yes, you are right… Just get in the water. Maybe then you will see what I already know to be true.

Ciara gestured to Jonathan. "Take off your clothes. You must enter the pool."

"Eh…that's sort of embarrassing," Jonathan argued.

Taylith shook his head. Nudity was not something the dragons had ever been embarrassed about. You did not enter the waters of the Clyss clothed.

"Suck it up, Jonathan. You've got nothing none of us haven't seen before," Laura called out to him.

"Do I even want these powers? Hell, I wouldn't know what to do with them." Jonathan began to walk back to the team.

Ciara called out after him. "Jonathan, you would anger the gods and goddesses? Worse, you would anger I Am? The greatest of them all?"

Jonathan stormed back to the pool. "Can the girls at least turn the other way?"

Taylith had already divested himself of his clothing and was waist deep in the pool when Jonathan finally undressed, hastening into the water to hide himself from view.

After they had reappeared and waded to the bank, Laura handed them both a towel. They quickly dried themselves and dressed.

"Thank you." Taylith gave Laura a quick kiss.

Jonathan screwed up his face. "I don't feel any different than before we got here."

Taylith slapped him on the shoulder. "Neither do I. Ciara and the others will help you learn how to use your power."

He was relieved his father had required that he train to use magick, even if his attempts had often failed.

"That bloody god scared the shit out of me."

Laura laughed. "Seems like even if you don't remember all those years, your mother's language rubbed off on you."

"We do speak kind of different, don't we?"

Taylith and Ciara walked to the clearing and changed to their dragons, ready to transport Niqine back to her village.

CHAPTER TWELVE

The flight to Niqine's village only took moments from leaving the Clyss. They landed on the ridge of the crater and waited while Ciara and Brenn escorted Niqine back to her home.

Where is this island, Ciara?

Rania will show us when we fly upward. It is directly above Xynnar.

Do you think Niqine will be safe now?

Yes. Rania told me the gods and goddesses have placed extra protection around the crater. She cannot leave without you or I flying her out, and if she wants to go to market, she will need to be escorted by one of us.

The market is quite empty now. Without produce to sell, many of the farmers are not setting up their stalls.

That is why we must find what Zohmes and Odoxon have placed on the island.

Brenn returned, interrupting their silent conversation. "Taylith, Ciara, upward!"

Taylith scanned the sky above him as he soared up. He saw nothing. Then suddenly, there were very dark clouds and a haze. He flew into it. Up ahead of them was the island. Strange, that from below the sky was clear.

Behold Storming Enclave.

I see it.

After scouting for a clear spot, they landed carefully. The island was dismal, its vegetation decayed. A heavy stench met their nostrils, like the reek of decomposing flesh.

Taylith shifted and quickly sought out Laura. "Please stay close to me while we are here. I don't want to lose you as I did in the temple."

"I am not leaving your side." She wrinkled her nose. "Nice place."

"It is hard to believe the island was once like the Tideless Abyss. Zohmes has done this, maybe with Odoxon's help."

"After what he did to Julia at the temple? Yes, Doxie baby would do something like this."

He scowled at her. "Baby? You call me that when we are together. Now you would call that sorcerer such?"

"Honey, I'm sorry. It's an Earth expression. It doesn't mean the same."

"Your Earth language is extremely puzzling."

"Sweetheart, if I call you baby, it's with love."

"But if you call Odoxon that?"

"It's definitely not with love." She stood on her tiptoes, kissed his lips, and grinned. "I kinda think it's cute when your eyes do that flashy thing."

Gods, the woman could be exasperating. Taylith twined his fingers with hers, then focused on their surroundings. "Look at the trees and vegetation."

"It's like something from a horror movie. If I didn't know better, I'd believe the whole area was diseased, but I have never seen anything like this."

Blackened trees surrounded them, their branches were gnarled and misshapen, the trunks covered in a sickly yellow fungus. The shrubbery on the ground was black and almost felt like charcoal beneath their feet. There was not a building in sight. All they could see was the dilapidated forest.

Aldis called them all together. "I have no idea where we are going. Ciara, do you have any directions to give us?"

Ciara shook her head. "No. We are on our own right now."

Ciara looked at Jonathan. "Jonathan, can you concentrate? You, too, Taylith? Maybe a vision will enlighten us."

Cewrick spoke up. "We need to move on straight ahead."

"How do you know, Father?" Icaras asked.

"I have a vague memory of this."

"Can your vague memory recall what Zohmes placed on this island?" Icaras pursued his questioning.

"Son, Zohmes possessed me for centuries. The memories of some things are vivid. Others, not too clear."

"Straight ahead it is." Brenn hoisted his backpack onto his shoulders and motioned for Cewrick to take the lead.

As they trudged forward through the charred blackness of the undergrowth, Taylith noted that the forest seemed to get thicker. The trees were larger, their branches stretching higher, the tips disappearing into the haze that blanketed the sky. The haze reminded him of a thick fog of smoke. The forest looked like it had been razed by dragon fire, the island drained of life. There was no evidence that it had once been a thriving city.

Laura brushed his shoulder, drawing his attention. "What do you think happened here? The forest looks as if it's been on fire, but there is no ash or soot."

Taylith gripped her arm to stop her when she reached out to touch one of the trees. "I do not know what magick affects the island. This was destroyed centuries before I was born." He urged her forward. "Come. We must not tarry too far behind the team."

Laura gazed up at him. Her eyes widened, the glow of his soul shard suddenly enveloping her body. "What in the hell is that thing!"

Taylith turned, pushing her behind him, and drew his sword. "Stay behind me."

A smoky mist curled from the trees, wraith-like creatures rising above it. Smoky hair billowed around featureless faces. Their cheeks were sunken, their teeth bared, and gaping holes appeared where the eyes should have been. Bones peeked through the pitch-black skin that covered their emaciated bodies. Long, skinny arms stretched out in front of them. The spiked fingers of their hands scraped against the tree trunks, gouging chunks of blackened bark from them. The wraiths advanced upon them in a wave of smoke and ash.

"Ooooh! You have got to be fucking kidding me!" Taylith heard Erica yell.

"Shield yourselves!" Astiana screamed.

One of the creatures shot forward, its legless body leaving a trail of fire on the already scorched ground. Taylith slashed it with his sword, the blade going clean through its abdomen. The monster's body dissipated, then reformed, whole once again.

Beside him, Laura fired her fleet weapon, shooting the wraith in the eye socket. Its head whipped back and a howl escaped its lipless mouth. Suddenly the inky blackness of its skin curled in upon itself. The creature disintegrated to ash.

Laura patted him on the arm. "Told you I was a damn sharpshooter."

"You were supposed to stay behind me," he hissed.

"Don't worry, baby, I got your back."

Taylith sheathed his sword and grabbed his fleet weapon, then yelled to the others, "Shoot them in the eye sockets!" He took aim and fired at the wraiths, Laura keeping pace beside him.

A chant rose above the sounds of the weapons. A loud

boom echoed through the forest, shaking the ground beneath their feet. Suddenly a flare of light flashed through the smoky mist, engulfing the wraiths in its radiance, then complete silence as the ash from their bodies rained upon the ground.

"The god of fire has stepped in to help us," Astiana said. "We are fortunate to have the gods and goddesses fighting on our side."

They trudged on through the dismal forest, being careful not to touch anything, until they came to the edge. Not far from where they stood was a ravine. A broken bridge dangled from frayed ropes. On the other side were ruins of what could have once been a castle or a temple. As far as they could see, the landscape resembled a war zone. Several statues lay broken on the ground.

They walked close to the craggy edge of the chasm. "This may have been a river," Taylith commented. "See the water lines on the sides?"

Taylith and Ciara were about to call out their dragons when Cewrick held up his hand. "Wait. Hear that sound?"

A loud rumbling, then a roar that shook the ground beneath their feet. They jumped back as something rose from the ravine. "It's a fucking giant!" Laura shouted.

Erica held her sword at the ready. "And not a fucking pretty one either!"

Taylith moved to shield Laura, but she promptly pushed her way back to stand beside him, her proton phaser and fleet weapon ready.

The head and shoulders appeared above the ravine. It had a deformed face, mangled ears, a solitary, glaring green eye in the center of a high forehead, and a mouth that reached from ear to ear. It was massive. Its body looked somewhat human, but yet it was not. It opened its mouth, gaping so large and wide, a whole house could disappear inside it. The monster could gobble up the whole team in one swoop. A long, forked tongue appeared from its mouth, snaking toward them. Large purple pulsing veins covered its head and upper body. Brenn and Erica hacked at the tongue with their swords. Taylith fired his proton phaser, but none of it did any good.

They had to jump to avoid the tongue, then ran back to the edge of the forest. It did not help. The tongue seemed endless, following them, flicking in and out of its grotesque mouth, attempting to snatch them. The creature rose further from the chasm until they could see it from the waist up. Its twin hearts were attached to each side of its body. Horns protruded from each shoulder. Sharp spikes jutted out from the arms. Its skin, if one could call it that, was a mottled gray.

"Retreat!" Aldis ordered.

Cewrick yelled, "No!"

Taylith watched in amazement as the sorcerer's body began to radiate a bright golden color. Within seconds, waves of yellowish beams emitted from him toward the giant, enveloping it. It roared. Its gigantic hands slammed against its ears. Another giant appeared from the chasm, and another, and more. The light enveloped all of them. They turned on one another, their tongues snaking, pulling, their horns puncturing heads, shoulders, chests, until the last one fell. With a final burst of flames, now issuing from Cewrick, Biryn, Ciara, Icaras, and Astiana's hands, the monsters crumbled. What was left of them tumbled into the ravine.

The radiance surrounding Cewrick's countenance turned blue. He chanted, then returned to normal. "Jump now!" he shouted.

"Jump?" Taylith wondered. "It's too wide."

"Holy shit. I feel something." Jonathan sprinted toward the edge and leaped. He landed safely on the other side.

Taylith picked Laura up and held her in his arms. "Hold tight."

She wrapped her arms around his neck and quickly kissed his cheek. "Don't drop me, studmuffin."

He raised a brow, not sure if he really wanted to know the meaning of the word. "Studmuffin?"

She grinned at him and winked. "It means that you are a sexually attractive guy with big bulging muscles."

He gave her a sidelong glance. "There is something seriously wrong with your Earth words."

"What... You got upset about the whole Doxie baby thing and I would never call that creature a studmuffin."

"I guess you have a point." He took a running leap across the ravine, making it safely to the other side, then placed Laura on her feet and steadied her.

Hesitantly, each of the team followed behind them.

"Did you bespell all of us, Cewrick?" Aldis asked.

"No. There are many things you can do now. Even Erica, Ivran, Laro, and you. Remember, before we traveled to Yanata, you were all, except Laura, given certain abilities. The gods have revealed what you all are able to do."

"And just what are they?" Erica demanded. "We still haven't been told. It would be nice to know that I can leap across such a space, jump from tall buildings, and whatever else."

"We can talk later," Brenn told them. "We must go on."

Cautiously, they approached the ruins. "I have a feeling we will find what we are looking for here." Taylith stealthily rounded the corner of what had once been a hallway.

A figure stood in the center of a large area, probably the main hall of the temple or castle. Its head resembled that of a bird, its body half human with misshapen hands and feet. Long, coarse hair floated in a halo effect around the head.

Behind it stood an urn on a pedestal. Greenish flames with curling red eel-like snakes dancing among it came from the mouth of the urn. Dark smoke spiraled upward, sideways, toward the sky, and into the island's atmosphere. Thick chains from his wrists bound the bird-like man to the solid rock ground. Its beak opened wide and it hissed at the interlopers. Black wings dotted with tiny green flames sprang from its back and spread wide.

"Zohmes and Doxie have been fucking busy creating all these monstrosities," Laura hissed.

The birdman began to glow fiercely until he turned into solid steel. Even the wings appeared to be made of metal.

Taylith edged forward. "I think only magick can defeat these apparitions. Our weapons barely touched them. Even our swords seem to be useless."

Laura yanked him back. "Then heaven forbid that war you mentioned will happen. Lord knows what their troops will consist of."

The monster wrenched the chains that bound it to the rock, breaking one of its arms free. Its incandescent gaze pinned them. It screeched menacingly and began to break the chain that bound its other arm. The grommet anchored into the rock started to loosen.

"Why the hell did it never break free if it can do so now?" Laura yelled.

They fired their proton phasers at the abomination. The shots were deflected by the steel armor that surrounded the creature's body. Great metal wings flapped ferociously on its back and it slammed its loose hand to the ground, rubble from the dilapidated walls raining down around them.

"I will try to hold it." Cewrick chanted and held his staff out in front of him, the crystal shining a bright gold.

"Join hands. Quickly!" Astiana exclaimed.

Icaras, Ciara, and Biryn linked hands with Astiana and joined in Cewrick's spell. Cewrick aimed his staff at the brute. Red bands of effulgent light wound tight around the birdman's body. It fell to the ground with a crash, its body effectively pinned.

"Hurry, you must use the four swords. Pierce its heart and sever its head!" Cewrick yelled above the chanting. "Jonathan, go with them, you will be needed to release the spell from the urn!"

Drawing his sword, Taylith raced with Brenn, Erica, Biryn, and Jonathan to the birdman. Taylith knew his sword was magical, had felt the power of it when he had been called upon to use it, but now that magick raged like a tempest through his body, the blade glittered brightly. When they reached the trapped creature, he noticed the other swords glowed as well.

"Biryn, Erica, pierce its heart. Brenn and I will sever its head."

Taylith placed his blade on the back of the creature's neck. Brenn's blade nestled in the front. They heaved their swords back and swung, slicing through the monster's neck like butter. The head clanged onto the ground and rolled away from the thrashing body. From the corner of his eyes, he could see Biryn and Erica stab their swords through the birdman's chest, piercing its heart. As soon as they removed their swords, the body began to gleam brightly, their blades turning the metal back to flesh. The wings now had feathers. The green fire that dotted the wings spread until the whole creature was a flaming green ball. Then it burst into a shower of sparks and melted into a small pool of molten steel.

Taylith turned his attention to Jonathan. "Your turn."

"What do you mean, my turn? I have no idea what I am doing!" Jonathan remarked, then turned toward the urn. "A little guidance, please. Anyone with experience on how to break a spell on a bedeviled urn is—"

Suddenly, Jonathan's face displayed an odd expression, almost like he was hypnotized. He started toward the urn, as if in a trance. Taylith reached out to stop him, concerned he was under a Zohmes or Odoxon's spell.

Jonathan brushed his hand away and continued forward. "I know what to do now."

Once Jonathan reached the urn, he knelt before it. He embraced it. The green fire flared bright, the dark smoke growing in thickness, enveloping Jonathan, hiding him from their view.

"Oh my God! The smoke is eating him! Do something!" Laura yelled and began toward the black cloud.

Taylith reached out to stop her, but no need. A booming voice chanted, eerily sounding like the voice of Zohmes, but much younger. "It appears Jonathan has found his magick."

Loud growls issued from the smoke stack. A fierce rumbling almost deafened them, resembling thunder. The chanting continued until the black smoke began to fade, turn white, then a faint rose and blue, and finally dissipated.

Taylith rushed to Jonathan, who sat on the ground, his arms still around the urn. "Are you all right?"

"Yes. Flabbergasted, but I think I'm fine."

He shook his head at yet another strange Earth word. In awe, Taylith saw the urn slowly turn a brilliant gold that sent a golden incandescence over them all and the surroundings. Around them, the island creaked and groaned as Jonathan's magick slowly restored its former beauty.

Laura joined them. She embraced Jonathan. "Nephew, I am so proud of you!" Then she turned to Taylith and briefly hugged him.

"That's enough, you two. Go get a room." Jonathan stood

and grinned widely down at them.

Arms around each other's waists, Taylith and Laura walked back to the team, followed by Jonathan.

"Jonathan, you are the first and only person from Earth to have real magical powers. I am thoroughly impressed," Erica said.

"I'm not completely from Earth, I guess. It's strange. I suddenly heard a voice that told me what I had to do."

Astiana nodded. "The gods and goddesses are guiding you. Soon, you will be as powerful as your father."

"Don't you ever call him my father again. In my opinion, he was nothing but a sperm donor."

Taylith pointed at their surroundings. "Look, we are standing in a temple, or maybe it's a palace. Everything is turning green, and flowers are blooming. It is much like the Tideless Abyss now. My parents can return to their original home."

"They must do so soon. War looms ahead. The dragons will be needed to help protect Xynnar Valley and the crystals. The koriam mines must not fall to Zohmes and Odoxon," Cewrick warned.

They walked out of the building and stood on the steps, gazing at the beauty before them. The ravine was now a gurgling, pristine river. Birds sang and waterfowl floated on the water. Flowers and green shrubbery flanked both sides. Where there was the broken bridge before, they saw a beautiful, stone bridge curving over the river, leading to the forest beyond.

"I believe we can return to the palace now. Let us all thank the gods and goddesses for their help and pray for peace from the two that mean us harm," Astiana told them.

"I could easily stay here for a while," Laura said, snuggling against Taylith. "It would be a great place to spend our honeymoon," she whispered.

Taylith and Ciara changed into their dragons. When the team was seated, they began their downward journey.

CHAPTER THIRTEEN

They were overjoyed when they briefly landed close to Xynnar and saw the vegetation once again lush and green. Taylith suspected that the crops in the hothouses were once again healthy, too.

He did not want to think about his vision and hoped they would have some respite from the sorcerer and Zohmes' attacks. Now that Laura had agreed to be his mate, he badly wanted some alone time with her.

Biryn called out. "Let us go to the palace and celebrate a successful mission."

"Sounds like a plan," Laura said. "I, for one, have to vote yet for the name of our realm. I think Erica does as well. I'll do it as soon as we're back. I can use my tablet to do it."

"Which name are you voting for?" Taylith asked.

"I'm not allowed to say. The king has to approve it first before anyone else can know. We can't even discuss it among ourselves. And then we have to vote in a leader, or ruler as you call it. There is already a list of names."

"Have you made up your mind about that one?"

"Yes. I wasn't forbidden to talk about that. I choose Bernie Henderson. He's still young, innovative, well-educated, an engineer, among many other things, and he's kind. He's also a very wise man. I think he will be a fine leader of our people. I really like him."

"That brings up a question. After the ceremony, where will you want to live? Now that I have enlisted in Biryn's troops, I cannot live on Storming Enclave. I need to be within on-call distance. That will make your new city too far away, too."

"We'll talk about it later. They're waiting for you to change again so we can fly back to the palace."

Taylith shifted into his dragon. He hoped silently that the living arrangement would not be a problem. They really had to live near the palace, close to Cront.

During the mission, they had not taken time out to eat. When the servants brought in dishes of delectable food, Taylith's stomach growled so loud, Laura nudged him.

He gave her a lopsided grin. "What? Flying makes you hungry."

Ciara nodded in agreement while filling her plate. "And we have done plenty of flying today."

Biryn took a sip of his wine. "Cewrick, you made mention of the koriam mines. The village of Xynnar was destroyed, its people captured. The Tronconians were taken as well, before Ciara, Rania, and Icaras banished you to Garissa Island. What was Zohmes' purpose. Do you remember?"

"The koriam crystals contain great magick. It was used in forging the four swords. The crystal of my staff is one of those crystals, a large one... And Odoxon's." Cewrick released a deep breath. "I know of the rumors that the ultimate weapon could be created using koriam crystals and the irorcan ore from the Tronconian mine. This is not the case. It is not the irorcan that the koriam reacts with."

"If this is true, then why capture the Tronconians?" Laro sat back in his chair, crossing his arms over his chest.

"To enlist the help of the rogue Tubosians, Zohmes offered them the irorcan ore. It is worth much on their planet."

Biryn rubbed his chin. "Yes, it is. I had only recently opened trade agreements with Empress Khatari before the kidnappings."

Ivran set his fork on his plate, a confused expression crossing his features. "If the irorcan ore is not the problem, then why is our technology unstable close to the mines?"

Cewrick scrunched his brows. "I am not sure, but I believe that the corruption of Storming Enclave and the binding of Jelano's powers affected the magick of the crystals. Even something as simple as a sun-powered cooler would become unstable." Cewrick gestured to the soul shard around Laura's neck. "The dragons created the koriam crystals. The best way to gain control of the magick of the land is by enslaving its guardians and healers. What Zohmes did not count on was Brenn and his ability to free Ciara from the Clyss. With the return of the jewel dragons, the land will heal and its magick will be protected from corruption."

Taylith studied Cewrick a moment. What the sorcerer had said was true. The jewel dragons did create the koriam. Before the curse, the dragons strengthened and replenished them during the season of frost. Like the soul shards, the dragons kept that secret close. Only the gods and goddesses knew of their ability. Zohmes would have had knowledge of it before his fall from grace. "By enslaving us, Zohmes thought to harness the power to create the koriam crystals. When he corrupted us, changed us into the black dragons, we became creatures of destruction. We no longer had the gift to create the koriam."

"What was he planning to do with the crystals?" Biryn asked.

Cewrick toyed with his glass, a worried expression

crossing his face. "The koriam he did obtain while he was in control of the mines is being used to forge weapons for his army. The crystals focus and strengthen the power of the person using them. They can be used for great good…or terrible evil."

Taylith nodded in agreement. "Zohmes and Odoxon have bespelled the weapons that are being forged. The army will not be easy to defeat."

Laura caressed his hand, twining her fingers with his. "Now that Jonathan has the same power as Zohmes, won't he be able to help counteract their spells like he did on Storming Enclave?"

Astiana looked at each one of them, her eyes filled with pain. "Zohmes has had centuries to set his plans in motion. His evil is entrenched within many of the realms, as you have seen in Sirona. We do not have the power to undo this evil overnight. Even with the help of his son."

Biryn wiped his mouth with his napkin. "Enough talk of Zohmes and Odoxon. Storming Enclave has been replenished. Our crops have been saved…" He gazed at Taylith and Laura, a grin suffusing his face. "And we have a joining ceremony to plan."

"But how—"

Biryn interrupted Laura and gestured to Astiana. "My great-grandmother is the goddess of love."

Julia chuckled. "Anyone with eyes can see the two of you are head over heels."

Laura squeezed Taylith's hand, then turned to Julia. "We were going to wait to announce our engagement. I didn't want to upset you after what you had been through."

"How could I be upset about your happiness?" Julia's eyes misted with tears. "I loved John and losing him is painful and raw. Even through the pain, I do not regret my choice. I would not have my son." She wiped the tears from her eyes and sniffled. "The goddess Rania gifted me with the memories of my pregnancy, Jonathan's birth, and the joy of raising him. I now have snapshots in my brain—of him in my arms, learning to walk, as a teenager, and becoming a young man."

"Anything else about the next twenty-four years?" Icaras asked eagerly.

"No, they're just images of Jonathan and the two of us. He was such a beautiful baby." She sighed, a tear trickling down her cheek.

"I wish I could look into your mind and take a peek at those images. I am finding it really weird that my nephew is older than I am," Laura said. "About our joining, Taylith and I just want something really quiet. No fanfare and big celebrations. Maybe just the team, a few close friends, and if Astiana could perform the joining?"

Ciara chuckled. "Remember Brenn and my ceremony? Yours and Taylith's has to be the same."

"No fucking way will I stand there naked and get painted!"

Taylith's heart sank. The cleansing ceremony was required by the gods to complete their joining. They had to enter the Clyss. "If I am to give you my soul shard completely, then we have to go through the traditional joining ceremony for dragons."

"Aunt Laura, if you love this man and want to marry him, you'll have to suck it up." Jonathan grinned.

Biryn stood and raised his glass. "It is decided. Your joining ceremony will be held in two days."

"Two days? That's not enough time to get a dress," Laura shrieked.

Taylith cleared his throat. "You can wear whatever you wish. There will be more guests than just the team, sweetness. My parents and Ciara's parents will need to be there to witness the event."

"I put my foot down about the painting stuff. I will not get naked, especially in front of your family. Are you kidding me? I haven't even met your folks." Laura became flustered.

"A dress is no problem, Laura. Your seamstress Olivia, and the palace seamstress can work fast. Yes, we can arrange this to take place in two days at the Clyss. It is getting late. Cylena, shall we retire?"

After the king and queen had left, Taylith and Laura went to their room. They undressed, Laura turning quickly to creep into Taylith's arms before he had a chance to go to the bathroom. "Hold me tight," she murmured against his neck. "Do we really have to get naked and painted in front of everyone?"

He cupped her chin, tilting it to gently kiss her. "The painting of our bodies has meaning. The gods and goddesses guide the attendants' hands as they paint, and for each couple the design is different. This is the first step of our joining. Then we must enter the Clyss to complete the ceremony." He traced his finger down her neck to the pendant nestled between her breasts. "Without this ceremony, we can never be truly joined. Your soul will not receive my shard."

"Then I will suck it up, even if I'm uncomfortable with it." She pressed closer against him, her arms winding around his neck.

Her naked body against his sent the blood pulsing through his veins. "Let's go and bathe?" she suggested.

"We already bathed before dinner."

"Not together."

His heart melted at her impish smile. "After you, jewel of my soul."

"Oh, that sounds so romantic. If I were a writer, I would use that in a book." She skipped ahead to the bathroom.

As always, perfumed water filled the large sunken tub. Fragrant flower petals drifted on the surface. Taylith waded down the steps and sat beside her. He pulled her over to sit in front of him, his cock throbbing with the need for her, now rubbing against her butt cheeks. He took a breast in each hand and massaged gently, tweaking her nipples into hard peaks. Her moan of bliss sent thrills through his body from his loins up to his stomach.

Laura turned suddenly and straddled him. Lifting her hips, she slowly sank onto his cock. The water bubbled between them as she began to move her hips up and down. Taylith drank in her beauty. Her head was flung back, her blonde locks cascading down her back. Her breasts, firm mounds with dusky rose nipples poking from light brown aureoles, set him on fire like never before.

Her movements increased in tempo. Oh, he wanted to take those alabaster mounds in his hands, suck those inviting nipples, but if he let go of her, she would fall backward.

When she reached behind him to clasp the edge of the tub, he had his chance. He crushed each breast in his hands, then bent to take a nipple in his mouth. Her hips moved faster still. He felt the blood pump in the veins on his cock, causing it to swell even more. He was so ready to come. She pressed her body against his, imprisoning his hands between them. He squeezed her breasts harder when her lips crashed on his, her tongue entering his mouth, exploring, dancing with his own.

Her body trembled, echoing his own imminent release. A shudder shook him as he felt his semen shoot through the channel of his cock into her.

Still trembling, they held each other until the fire within them was somewhat doused. Taylith knew it would not take long for him to become erect again.

Laura finally let go of him. Reaching behind him, she

produced the flask of perfumed soap. Pouring some into her hand, she began to lather him with it. "Laura, sweetness, at this rate we will spend the night in water."

Her grin was infectious. He chuckled. "Is that what you want?"

"And turn into a prune?"

"Mm, what is a prune?"

"I'd come out of the water looking like a hundred-year-old woman."

"Oh, you mean a zonomi fruit."

She laughed, the tinkling sound acting like balm on his heart and soul. "Whatever you call it here. Wash me, baby."

"I think I like studmuffin better. Now can you explain in more detail exactly what that means?"

"Mm, a stud is a muscular man. It is also the term for a male horse. Muffin is a sweetish cake we eat for breakfast on Earth."

"I am not sure I like being compared to a horse. But anything is better than feeling like an infant." Taylith soaped her, taking especially long on the area between her legs. His cock was ready for her again, his blood coursing through his veins. Gods, she was turning him into an insatiable lunatic driven to make love to her. "Let us take this to the bed now? After today, we do need to sleep a few hours."

"Uh-uh, we can sleep after I rid you of this." Her hand closed around his cock and moved the skin back and forth.

He groaned, stood, and scooped her up against his chest. Dripping wet, he deposited her on the bed and took her into his arms.

CHAPTER FOURTEEN

The two days before their joining had flown by so fast, Taylith could hardly believe he stood in the Clyss, waiting for his soon-to-be mate.

The king and queen, his and Ciara's parents, and the team were present as well as some of Laura's Earth friends. Julia and Jonathan would stand in the place of Laura's parents to give the permission for the joining. When Brenn's flyer landed, he waited impatiently for her to disembark.

Gods, she was beautiful. When her gaze caught his, her green eyes glowed with joy. A fur cloak in the deepest emerald-green was draped across her shoulders. The edges, hem, and hood were embroidered in silver thread depicting elaborate foliage and ferns. His breath caught in his throat when she slipped it from her shoulders and handed it to Julia. Her simple white gown fell in graceful folds down to her ankles, her shoulders were bare, the bodice cut in a deep "v" open to her waist. A tie encrusted with green gems wrapped around her body from beneath her breasts, all the way to her waist. A translucent shimmering white veil covered her golden-blonde hair, held by a coronet of green fern, its edges sparkling with the same green gems that encircled her waist.

Jonathan led her to stand beside him, then joined Julia on

the silvery sand beside the pool.

Taylith twined his fingers with hers, his gaze searching her face for any hint of nervousness. There was not any. Her face was filled with happiness and her eyes shone with love. He squeezed her hand. *I love you, sweetness. Are you ready for this?*

She inclined her head. *I love you, too, studmuffin. Let's do this before I lose my nerve. The only one I wish to get naked in front of is you.*

They turned their attention to Astiana as she approached. The goddess raised her hands into the air, her face turned to the sky. "May the gods and goddesses smile upon you both this day. As the goddess of love, I will now unite you both, one to the other."

Julia and Jonathan approached. Astiana turned her attention to them. "Julia and Jonathan of Earth, do you give your permission for Laura to join with Taylith, prince of Storming Enclave. Do you welcome him into your family?"

"We do." They spoke as one.

"Laura of Earth, do you wish to be joined with Taylith, prince of Storming Enclave?"

"Yes, I do."

"Taylith, prince of Storming Enclave, do you wish to take Laura as your eternal mate?"

"I do."

They bowed their heads as Astiana draped a wreath of vines and leaves around their necks. "Just as this wreath encircling your necks, the love you have for one another has been forged with strength. Honor that love. Treasure it above all things and be true to the bond that is alive within you. By my authority as the goddess of love, you are now mated for all eternity. Now, you will complete the purification ceremony."

Taylith gazed at Laura before he began to divest himself of

his uniform. Her hands trembled as she took the jeweled tie of her gown in her fingers. He tried to calm her. *Focus on us, my jewel. There is nobody here but us.* His shard began to softly glow, and the shaking of her hands ceased.

She peeked up at him. *What did you do? The nervousness is gone and I feel at peace... A prince? They're kidding, right?*

He shrugged. *Hurry and undress. I don't want to wait any longer to make you mine.*

They quickly divested themselves of their clothing and turned to face each other. Taylith's attention focused on Laura as the women began to paint. The design was exquisite. Green ferns and foliage took shape, with bursts of colorful flowers. His lady love transformed into the beautiful land of their planet. He heard a gasp escape her lips and her soft voice in his mind. *Taylith, your design, it's stunning! Flames encircle a golden sword, the stars and comets...a planet. You are the fire burning in the sky above Ierilia.*

And you are the land lush with life.

The rumbling of thunder shook the ground beneath their feet after the paintings were complete. A bolt of lightning crashed to the ground. Before them, the everchanging countenance of I Am appeared.

"Taylith, prince of Storming Enclave, you are a guardian of the land, a powerful sorcerer in your own right. Laura, you are a healer of the land and the keeper of souls. You both have proven the brightness within you through the trials and tribulations of your captivities."

I Am pinned Taylith with his everchanging stare. "Taylith, you will guard and protect this woman I have chosen for you. The powers I gift her with now, will save the lives of many, for she has the ability to anchor the dying to life and the power to replenish the beauty of the land."

A shower of sparking mist reigned from the sky,

enveloping Laura in a colorful glow. Slowly the light receded and I Am continued. "Laura, you have been chosen as the eternal lifemate of my chosen vessel, the keeper of my prophesies, and a protector of the crown. I anoint this union with my blessing. May the strength of your love guide you. You may both now enter the Clyss so the waters may cleanse you of the past and bless the union of your souls."

I Am's countenance slowly dissipated in a shower of sparks. Taylith led Laura to the banks of the basin, his soul shard glowing brightly as they entered the water together and waded beneath the surface. A flare of light so bright he had to close his eyes sheltered them within its heat. Tendrils of power snaked around him, sinking beneath his skin, shredding him apart. He gasped as the soft caress of Laura's essence joined his, the power building to an inferno as it knitted its intricate weave. Two souls reformed, two lives eternally entwined... And the magick he was born to wield coursed through his veins.

The glow subsided. The joining was complete. Taylith helped a dazed Laura to the banks of the Clyss, both quickly donning the robes waiting for them. Laura reached to touch the pendant, then gave him a confused look when she discovered it was no longer there.

"What happened to it?" Worry laced her tone.

He traced his finger down her cheek, to her neck, then placed his palm over her heart. "The shard is now a part of your soul as it is a part of mine."

The king and queen were the first to congratulate them. "May the gods and goddesses bless you both." Biryn embraced Laura, then Taylith.

Cylena followed with her wishes for them. "May your union be fruitful and your love as pure as the love Biryn and I bear each other."

Taylith's parents were next, followed by Ciara's parents.

Copera first hugged Taylith, then Laura. "We welcome you into our family, Laura. We are so happy Taylith has met the lifemate chosen for him by the gods." A fleeting expression of sadness crossed her features before quickly fading away. "I have always longed for a daughter."

Copera grasped his hands and smiled. Taylith wondered. Had he imagined her sadness? Did it bother her that much that she never had a daughter?

Jelano clapped Taylith on the shoulder and kissed Laura on the cheek. "You must visit soon. We look forward to getting to know our new daughter."

After King Brokig and Queen Iede wished them well, Biryn turned and announced, "Now off to the palace to celebrate."

The guests proceeded to the waiting flyers. Julia and Jonathan were waiting for them near theirs. When they were the last ones left standing beside the Clyss, Laura quickly put on her dress and Taylith his uniform. After they were dressed, she stood on her toes and kissed him. "I can't believe we're man and wife. Is this real? Or am I dreaming?"

"You are not dreaming, my princess."

"I am a princess now?"

"Yes, sweetness, jewel of my heart and soul. My princess. Come, they are waiting for us." Taking her hand, they walked to the flyer.

Julia embraced them both. "I've never seen you happier, Laura."

"Aunt Laura, you look absolutely breathtaking," Jonathan complimented.

Taylith looked out the window as they approached the palace and were about to land. "I was afraid of that."

"Afraid of what?"

"Look for yourself."

Laura turned to peek out of the window. "Oh my God! How many people did Biryn and Cylena invite? And we wanted it to be small? Quiet?"

Taylith grimaced. "There is no arguing with Biryn. I imagine my aunt and uncle and parents had a hand in the guest list as well."

After they descended, Taylith worriedly draped the cloak closer around Laura and pulled her hood up against the falling snow.

They were the last to enter the ballroom. All the people from Earth were there. "The staff must have worked like crazy to get all this ready in time," Taylith remarked.

The ballroom was decorated with ferns and hothouse flowers. Tables laden with fowl, fruit, cheese, breads, and vegetables stood ready.

Laura took in a deep breath and groaned. "Everything smells so wonderful. I'm suddenly starving."

The team was seated next to the royal couple. There were two empty decorated chairs. "I guess those are our seats." Taylith pulled her along among shouting and clapping.

"Geez, my people alone count to about two hundred. Small wedding indeed," Laura whispered close to his ear.

"I suppose the king misunderstood. Our ceremony was quiet. You never mentioned the feast. Too late now. Let us enjoy this special day that happens only once in a lifetime."

"I hope there'll be no speeches. You know how I hate sitting through those?"

Taylith grinned. "Nothing we can do about it. In your language, suck it up."

Biryn picked up the bell and stood, then swung it back and forth. The buzz quieted and everyone waited for him to speak.

"Welcome to all of you and thank you all for being here to

join Taylith and Laura in their happiness. This is a very special day. Never in the history of Ierilia has a dragon mated with an alien. It was special enough when my general, Brenn, mated with a dragon and when Laro, a lion shifter, mated with Erica from Earth. But Brenn and Laro were born and raised on Ierilia. For the gods and goddesses, the book of knowledge, to have chosen an Earth mate for Prince Taylith, a jewel dragon of Storming Enclave, is highly unusual.

"Taylith and Laura, the queen and I wish you many years of joy and love. May your union bear fruit and unite Earth's people with those of Ierilia. Let us toast to their everlasting happiness!" Biryn raised his goblet and held it high.

They all raised their glasses and toasted. Suddenly, the ballroom echoed with the clattering of forks on plates. "What is this?" Biryn demanded. "I remember the guests doing the same at Erica and Laro's celebration."

Bernie Henderson stood. "Your Majesty, on Earth, if guests tap on their plates with their fork or knife, it means they want the couple to kiss."

Laura's face flushed pink. "Oh my God!"

Taylith stood, pulled her up, took her into his arms, and kissed her soundly.

Biryn continued. "I think I like this Earth tradition. Now, since we have already shocked the couple enough by organizing the festivities, after they requested a small gathering, let us eat."

After they had finished dining, the orchestra began to play. Taylith led Laura to the ballroom for the first dance.

He pulled her into his embrace and kissed the tip of her nose. "Are you happy, love?"

She wrapped her arms around his neck, her green eyes sparkling. "Yes, oh yes. But I'll be happier when I can be alone with you. This has surpassed any wedding that could have happened on Earth." She chewed on her bottom lip. "But I need to be honest with you. I was really nervous before I arrived at the Clyss. I was afraid that you wouldn't show up."

"Aw, sweetness. How could you ever have doubted I would not be there? But I understand." He grinned and swirled her around the dance floor. "You are stuck with me now."

They had no option but to admire their gifts and spend time talking to the guests. Deep down, Taylith just wanted to scoop her up and fly off with her, but they had to follow protocol.

It was close to midnight when she leaned heavily against him. "My feet are killing me. I can't believe how much I've danced tonight."

"I think we can safely disappear now. Let us thank Biryn and Cylena for arranging this and go to our room."

After thanking Biryn and Cylena, he quickly ushered Laura to their room and opened the door for her.

She hesitated a moment. "On Earth, a husband carries his bride over the threshold. But this isn't our house. You can do that when we have our own home."

"Threshold?"

"Through the door into our home."

"Oh. Well, I can do it anyway." He smiled from ear to ear, scooped her up, and kicked the door open.

Their room smelled heavenly of burning incense. Candles stood everywhere, and there were vases filled with flowers on all the tables and nightstands. He stood her beside the bed, then undid the emerald-green strings that held her dress, slipped it off her shoulders until it whispered to the floor and she stood naked before him. "I'm almost sorry the beautiful paintings on your body disappeared in the waters of the basin."

"Yes, same with yours. You looked so handsome, my prince. Otherworldly. If I'd only had a camera, well, my tablet at least."

"I am sure someone recorded our ceremony." He wasted no time, wrapping his arms around her and lowering her to the bed. "Would you like some wine, sweetness?"

"Are you kidding? I've been waiting for this since we got painted!"

CHAPTER FIFTEEN

Three weeks of blissful peace. Taylith could hardly believe it. Nothing had happened at their ceremony or the celebration, and he and Laura had been able to fly to Storming Enclave and spend time with his parents. Then they had gone to a secluded beach in a warmer part of Ierilia and enjoyed their honeymoon.

Much to their surprise, Biryn and Cylena had gifted them with an estate of their own, close to Cront. Once owned by the jewel dragons, the property had fallen to the crown after the dragons were cursed by Cewrick. They had been busy the last week overseeing restoration, remodeling, and painting. Today was the day they were to move into their own house.

Laura squealed and erupted into giggles when Taylith picked her up and carried her through the front door of their new home.

She wrapped her arms around his neck and kissed him soundly. "You remembered!"

He lowered her to the floor, his arms encircling her waist. "I remember everything you tell me." Leaning down, he nipped her bottom lip. "We can start a family here."

She gave him a sidelong look. "Hey now, don't get ahead of yourself. I'm not ready to get pregnant. Look at what happened to Julia."

He burst out in laughter. "But I am not Zohmes."

She raised a delicate brow. "And neither am I ready to be a mother yet."

"We cannot stop what is written, Laura." He twisted a lock of her silky hair around his finger. "Besides, it could be centuries before the gods and goddesses bless us with a child."

Her eyes widened in shock. "Wait…what do you mean by centuries? When Ciara explained what a lifemate was, I didn't think to ask her about babies. And the king arranged our ceremony so fast!"

He released the lock of her hair and caressed her cheek. "When you received my soul shard, your physiology changed. It is now much like a dragon's. You will live just as long as I will, and your reproductive system will be dormant until the gods and goddesses choose to allow us a child."

She scrunched her face at him. "So…when we do procreate, will I bear little dragons? How do they come out, as dragons with little claws? Or do I lay eggs?"

He shook his head and chuckled. "Enough talk. How about we go and do some procreating, as you call it."

Laura giggled. "Silly. The painters are all over the house. They're almost done. And the furniture and stuff is arriving soon."

He leaned down and whispered against her lips. "They are finished painting in our room." Just as he kissed her, his communicator went off. Groaning, he fished it out of his pocket, glanced at the screen, and frowned. "We've been called to the palace for an urgent meeting."

She sighed. "Zohmes at it again?"

"Brenn did not say. Just that we have to go to the palace immediately."

"That doesn't bode good. I've got a sick feeling of dread in the pit of my stomach."

They were the last ones to arrive. Taylith took in the serious expressions on everyone's faces. He pulled out a chair for Laura, then sat next to her. "Need I ask?"

"Another part of your vision has come to pass." Biryn looked somber.

Brenn stood, his features hardened, his demeanor that of the general of the king's army. The only outward sign of his anger was the muscle twitching in his jaw. "Now that everyone is here... A report has come in from our outpost in Sirona. Zohmes has accumulated a large army. His troops have marched through many realms on Ierilia and are advancing through Sirona as we speak and leaving a trail of destruction. He and Odoxon are bespelling the men from the villages to join his militia. The Yeavoth have allied with him and have amassed their army alongside Zohmes' troops. They are heading toward our realm. He is killing the people that show opposition."

"Why are we only hearing about this now? Izarus warned us that the Yeavoth had joined Zohmes, but why?" Biryn wondered.

Aldis swiped his hand across the screen of his datapad. "Reports have it that Dronko is angry he has not received the technology we promised him. The raiding of villages has only just begun. The captain at our outpost in Sirona contacted Brenn immediately."

Taylith shook his head. "Does it matter why the Yeavoth have joined Zohmes and Odoxon?" He clenched his jaw. So many had lost their lives over the centuries for Zohmes' plan to come to fruition. "Zohmes has quietly gathered men from all over Ierilia for centuries to build his army. His minions have poisoned the minds of many against the king. He will use the innocents he has bespelled first before unleashing his creations."

Erica snorted. "No wonder Zohmes has been quiet. He has been too busy planning this desperate attack on the throne."

Aldis set his datapad on the table and took a deep breath. "Biryn, you need to make a decision. We cannot allow Zohmes' troops to reach Cront. And we must stop the destruction. It is time to call up our warriors and stop this war."

"I abhor the thought of the casualties, but we have no other choice. Make it so. We march at first light." Biryn stared pointedly at the women. "No women. I will not allow you to be injured, or worse…killed."

Taylith crossed his arms over his chest and gave Biryn a hard look. "Biryn, you need to stay here for the same reasons. We cannot risk the crown. I will call upon the jewel dragons to guard the palace and protect you and Cylena."

Astiana tapped her fingers on the table, gaining their attention. "This is a war we cannot win with mere weapons. It is a war against a sorcerer with mighty powers and against an even more powerful god. It must be fought with the help of magick. The only ones of the team to stay behind are Cylena and Hirsuta. We must go with you."

Erica scowled. "There is no way in hell I'm staying here. I might not have magic, but I can damn well wield my magic sword! And I'm a sharpshooter!"

Astiana nodded. "Yes, all four swords must go."

"I guess it has been decided for me." Biryn stood, his features grim. "Brenn, gather your troops. All of you, go and enjoy this evening and get ready to leave at first light." He took Cylena's hand and left the table.

Laura grabbed Taylith's arm. "I will not be left behind. I

am a better shot than Erica, and I have a gut feeling that I need to go with you."

"Sweetness, I do not want you to go with us. You are not trained for a war like this one promises to be."

Laura shook her head vehemently. "I never heard Astiana say I couldn't. She only mentioned Cylena and Hirsuta's names. Yes, I'll be fighting by your side."

Taylith took in the determined look on her face. *Stubborn woman. We will discuss this later.* He turned his attention back to the others.

Ivran sat back in his chair, his face a mask of worry. "Aldis, besides the converted villagers and the Yeavoth, do you have an idea how many troops Zohmes has amassed?"

Aldis' lips formed a tight, grim line. "From what my contact told me, they are in the thousands and many are armed with proton phasers and fleet weapons. There has to be a traitor in our midst. Otherwise, how would they get their hands on those weapons?"

Brenn scowled. "The arsenal is heavily guarded. I have not heard anything about stolen weapons. They must have raided the factory. But that would have been reported. It does not make sense."

"Or got the information from our computers and produced them," Laro suggested.

Aldis grunted. "In whatever manner they got the weapons, they have them. As well as bespelled swords, spears, axes, and bows and arrows."

"In light of this situation, will it be safe for our families to remain in Cront?" Erica asked.

Taylith understood her fear. He held the same for Laura and had talked to his father about the impending war. "Your families are welcome to stay at Storming Enclave under my parents' protection. They will not allow them to come to harm."

"Thank you, Taylith."

"Are we traveling in hovercrafts?" Laura wondered.

"Only to the stables. Horseback from there. Some of our warriors, the captains, will ride in on their horses. Your uniforms and weapons will await you here at the palace. I will see all of you, or most of you, before daybreak," Brenn told them.

Taylith and Laura followed the others as they left the king's quarters, all of them ready to return to their homes.

"Is Biryn's army large enough?" Laura asked when they reached the courtyard.

Taylith shifted into his dragon and kneeled for Laura to mount his back. *Yes, it is. But I stand firm. You will not go with me.*

She stood in front of him, nose to nose, and glared at him. "Like bloody hell I won't! You can't stop me. You're not the boss of me, even if we are married."

I will not have you risk your life.

"Oh? But you'll risk yours?" She shook her head and climbed onto his back, settling herself at the base of his neck. He sighed as she caressed his neck. *I love you, Taylith, and I have just as much at stake as you do in this. I'm not staying behind.*

I love you, too, my jewel. I will not chance losing you. He leaped into the air and spread his wings. Both were quiet for the duration of their flight home. He landed in the courtyard of their estate. After Laura had dismounted, he shifted back to his human form and took her into his arms. "This is our last night together for the gods know how long. Let us not quarrel?"

She gazed up at him, her face a mask of determination. "This is an argument you won't win. I stand firm."

"As do I."

"You are not about to get all medieval on me. We'll talk again in the morning. I'd rather make this night special instead of butting heads." She stood on her tip toes and kissed the firm line of his lips.

He growled and lifted her into his arms, kissing her soundly, then teased her bottom lip with his teeth. Gods, she drove him crazy. *Stubborn, stubborn woman.* "Then we shall leave this subject for the morning."

He carried her through the front door, kicked it shut behind them, and made his way up the stairs to their suite.

Laura turned the knob, pushed the door open, and squealed. "Oh my God! We have a bed and it's beautiful!"

Beautiful? Taylith scowled. It was pink… Lots and lots of pink bedding, and lace spilling from the canopy, the pink sheets and rose-decorated covers draping down the sides of the bed to the floor. The windows were covered in the same froth of pink. Even the walls were painted a pale rose. At least the marble floor tiles were white, with barely the hint of some pink veins. It reminded him of Ciara's room at her father's castle. "If you say so, sweetness."

Even with all the fluff and lace, he was thankful that the staff had prepared the room for them while they were away at the palace. He wanted nothing more than to crawl into their bed and lose himself in Laura's arms.

She grinned at him, her eyes sparkling with mirth. "I do say so. Ciara helped me pick it out."

He shook his head and grimaced. "Remind me to thank her later for her decorating assistance."

He nudged the door shut and carried her to the bed, lowering her to the floor in front of the soft, pink confection.

She slipped her arms around his waist and looked up at him. "Make love to me, Taylith. I don't want to think about what tomorrow will bring."

He pulled her close, crushing her lips in a demanding kiss. She moaned, opening her mouth for his assault. Her hands slid down his back to the base of his tunic. She grabbed the edge and tried to tug upward, then growled in frustration when she could not pull it off.

"Patience, my jewel. We have all night," he whispered against her lips. He stepped out of her embrace, took the base of her top in his hands, and helped her remove it. Gods, she was beautiful. All alabaster skin, glowing in the pale light of the moons that filtered through the windows. Her honey-blonde hair spilled over her shoulders, long enough now to brush the top of her pert breasts. He could not resist cupping them in his hands and teasing the hard points of her nipples.

She groaned, her hands tunneling under his tunic. "Your turn."

He yanked his tunic over his head, then backed her up against the post of the canopy. Taking her hands in his, he lifted them over her head. "Hold on to the post."

She did as he asked and gazed up at him, her green eyes sparking with passion. "God, Taylith. I ache... I need..."

Her hunger flared across their bond, inflaming his own desire. He traced his fingers from her hands, down her arms, to her chin. Tilting her head up, he leaned down, seeking her lips with his, then blazed a trail with his lips from the silky skin of her neck to the lush fullness of her breasts. A sigh escaped her when he took first one nipple, then the other in his mouth. He teased and tasted until her body trembled and one hand dropped to the back of his head, her fingers fisting in his hair. He stopped long enough to peer up at her. Her head rested against the canopy. Those beautiful green eyes were closed, and she worried her bottom lip with her teeth.

She groaned and tried to push him back toward her breasts. "Don't stop now."

144

Taylith chuckled. "Put your hands back up or I might just tie them in place."

Her eyelids snapped open, raw hunger radiating through their bond. *Interesting*. He would have to file that reaction for later use.

She returned her hand to the pole. "Keep teasing, baby. I can give just as good as I get."

He grinned. "I am looking forward to it."

Satisfied that she would keep her hands in place, he returned his attention to the creamy skin before him, her soft concave belly, the flare of her hips. He gripped the waist of her pants and tugged them down her legs, lifting each foot to remove them. Gently parting her thighs with his hands, he continued his exploration. When he took the nub of her clit between his teeth, then sucked, shudders wracked her body, and her cries of ecstasy filled the air.

He shifted up, lingering long enough to kiss her stomach, between her breasts, then her lips. Her arms circled his neck and she leaned her body against him a moment, then gazed up at him and smiled.

"My turn."

She twisted and pushed him toward the bed. He sat on the edge, pulling her down in his lap to straddle his legs. Her lips met his, her teeth teasing his bottom lip and her hands branding a trail of fire down his chest and abdomen. She grabbed the string at the front of his pants, releasing his aching cock. He groaned as her hand wrapped around his erection and she stroked from tip to base, then lifted her hips and impaled herself in one thrust. Need clamped him like a vice. He grasped her hips, meeting her movements thrust for thrust, his name whispered against his lips as she took him over the edge into ecstasy.

He kissed the tip of her nose. "I lov—"

The bed creaked, then shifted. A leg gave way, the mattress now hanging crooked on the floor. The canopy swayed above them.

Giggles erupted from Laura as Taylith quickly reacted and pulled her off the bed to safety before the canopy collapsed completely.

She sighed, then stood on her tiptoes and kissed him on the cheek while the canopy tumbled onto the bed into a heap of rose ruffles and lace. "I love you, too, studmuffin." She peered over his shoulder at the collapsed bed. "I think someone forgot a few screws when putting it together. We'll have something to remember this night and laugh about it when we're old and gray."

He laughed, then shoved the mattress to the floor and across the room for them to use temporarily to sleep on. It was much better than bedrolls on the tiled floor.

The clash of swords echoed through the mountains. Bodies littered the blood-stained ground. Giant men, their skin inky black, charged. Spears soared through the air.

A flash of light illuminated a woman's form. Laura kneeling beside a man on the ground, a gaping wound in his chest, a spear protruding from it, his lifeblood draining steadily. A myriad of colored sparks surrounded them. Laura placing her hands over the wound, attempting to stop the flow of blood. Laura removing the spear. The huge wound closing, the man's body now whole. Ivran's head turning to face him. Laura moving to another injured warrior, placing her hands on his wounds.

Taylith jerked awake, startling Laura. She rubbed her eyes sleepily. "What's wrong? Is it time to leave?"

"Nothing, sweetness." He kissed the top of her head. "No, we still have a little time. You get some more rest. I'll make us some coffee."

She sighed and snuggled under the blankets.

He left their temporary bed, then quickly bathed and dressed. The vision played over and over in his mind as he made his way downstairs to the kitchen. He had not really thought about the gifts I Am had bestowed upon Laura. He should have. They were important. If Laura did not go with them, he knew Ivran would die, and he would never permit that to happen. Ciara would be there, a little voice told him, But the vision had made it clear that it was Laura who saved Ivran's life. He had no choice but to allow her to go with them.

To his surprise, his staff was already busy in the kitchen and had prepared breakfast. He must have slept later than he thought. He grabbed two cups and a tray, poured the coffee, fixed a plate of food, and grabbed a fork. He would ensure Laura ate before they left for the palace, but he had lost his appetite.

After he made it back to their suite, he placed the tray on the table. He glanced up as Laura entered the room, toweling her hair.

"Mmm… Coffee…"

He pulled a chair out for her. "Sit and eat. We don't have much time before we have to leave for the palace."

She glanced up at him in surprise. "What? No argument? Just like that you change your mind about me going?"

He sat in the opposite chair and took a sip of his coffee. "I was given another vision." He explained what I Am had shown him, but he did not tell her all of it. To tell her of Ivran could alter the outcome.

"That's crazy! I don't have any of that kind of power."

He took a deep breath and set his cup on the table. "Now you do. Remember what I Am told us at the Clyss. And now the vision showed me you have the gift of healing."

She scrunched up her face. "Was that what happened

147

when your god showered me in sparkles?"

He nodded. "When we entered the Clyss, I Am's gift was completed, along with the joining of our souls."

She took a small bite of her eggs. "I can't eat this. I'm not at all hungry. Hey, I didn't bring it up at the meeting, but wouldn't it be better if Biryn sent his space fleet to annihilate Zohmes' army?"

"No. Too many innocent lives would be lost. The spaceships carry weapons that cause major destruction."

"It's going to take days, weeks, to march to Sirona. We have to cross mountains, and —"

"That is how wars are fought on Ierilia. Many of the warriors will be on foot. The officers will be on horseback. And the women of course."

"How many female warriors are there?"

"Until Erica, none. Only men become warriors. Our wars are too violent and bloody."

"I still can't wrap my head around your medieval ways and your futuristic technology, the vast difference between the two. It's like living on two different worlds all wrapped up into one."

"Ierilia has not experienced a war of this scale for centuries."

"From what I've learned of Ierilian history, centuries ago there were always wars. But didn't Brenn return from one not that long ago? That's when he found our first ship, the Initiation Five."

"That was a war between two lords. Small scale. You heard what Aldis told us. Zohmes has been spreading discontent across Ierilia. This war is world-wide. Are you ready to leave for the palace?"

148

CHAPTER SIXTEEN

After changing into their battle gear, Taylith and Laura headed for Biryn's quarters. He noticed everyone, except Brenn and Ciara, already seated around the breakfast table. Their faces were somber. Like he and Laura, none of them were eager to go on this mission. If one could even call it a mission. They were going into battle, and a major one at that. "Morning, everyone," he greeted as he pulled the chair out for Laura, then sat next to her.

The table was set with a hearty breakfast. He helped himself to meats, cheese, and bread, though he still had little appetite. Noticing that Laura was not touching the food, he nudged her. "You have to eat, sweetness. Our journey will be a difficult one and you will need all your strength."

"Taylith, I do not think it is a good idea for Laura to go with us," Biryn told him.

"She must. I do not want her to go, but I had a vision this morning that she has to go along."

"If the gods granted you a vision, then so be it."

Brenn and Ciara joined them, followed by Julia. Brenn remained standing. "Morning, my fellow warriors, ladies. Before I sit down to eat, I think we need to all stand and pray to the gods and goddesses. Biryn?"

Biryn nodded, pushed his chair back, and stood. "Thank you, General. Please join hands and raise them?"

Taylith clasped Laura's hand and Jonathan's, then raised them. They stood in silence for a few moments, each lost in their own prayer, until Biryn spoke.

"God of war, Zeemanko, we call upon you to guide and lead us. Give us the wisdom to plan our strategies, to deal with the enemy, and the strength to endure the hardships we must face. Lead us into battle and keep us safe from harm. Help us to return home victorious. We call upon all the gods and goddesses to watch over our loved ones, watch over the people of Ierilia, the women and children left behind, and keep them safe from the enemy's mighty roar."

Taylith watched as Biryn laid his hand on Cylena's swelling belly. "Please watch over my queen and little prince."

It had to be really hard for the king. It was difficult for all of them, but those left behind would be waiting in fear of never seeing their loved ones again.

Brenn cleared his throat. "Sit, everyone. Be sure to enjoy this breakfast, as it is the last one of such you will have for a while. Most of you have never seen battle and endured the hardships of a warrior, especially the women. There are no words to explain to you what we will face."

"If it is anything like the medieval wars I learned about that happened on Earth centuries ago, I have a fair idea," Erica said.

Laura agreed with her. "Yes, and what they portrayed in movies, but it is different to learn about them in history and watching a glorified movie battle than actually participating in a real war."

"Is there any chance that I can go?" Julia asked.

"Definitely not," Jonathan told her.

"But Laura can?"

Taylith cleared his throat. "You heard me earlier. The gods showed me that she must, Julia."

"But why?"

"I cannot explain, but we have to trust the gods."

Aldis stood. "I trust you are all wearing your skin suits? It will be much colder in the mountains. The women will ride with us. We will surround them at all times. Yes, even you, Erica."

Brenn's chair scraped on the floor as he stood as well. "I have received word that our troops are ready and waiting for us. If we are all finished, please get your swords, your backpacks, and coats. The hovercraft is waiting to take us to the barracks."

"Where are they located?" Laura asked Taylith.

"Outside of Cront." Taylith took her hand and they hurried to their room.

Laura put on the heavy leather fur lined coat and her warming gloves. "Do I really need to wear this thing? It's heavy and awkward. How can we fight wearing it? The damn armor is uncomfortable enough. And this helmet feels like a brick on my head."

"You will be sitting on a horse, love, so you will get cold easily, even with the skin suit. The men will be fighting, not the women."

"Right. Like I'm going to just sit and watch. No way in hell."

"Laura, I have a good mind to leave you behind if you keep talking that way. I have never fought in a war, but I can imagine it will be a bloody battle. You must obey Brenn and Aldis' orders at all times, or I will have you escorted home." Deep down he knew he could not do that, not after what the vision had shown him.

She saluted. "Yes, sir!"

The craft landed, and they descended the steps to the snow-covered ground. Twelve horses stood ready and waiting for them.

"Where is Atom?" Laro asked Brenn as they approached the horses.

"I left him at home in the stables. The risk of him getting hurt is too great this time," Brenn said as he took the reins of a black stallion.

Taylith helped Laura mount, then climbed onto the saddle of his gray. Brenn led the way to the troops. He held up his hand, stopping them, and turned the horse so he could face his warriors.

Taylith could not help but admire him. Brenn was an imposing figure at the best of times, but as a warrior, he was something else to behold.

Brenn raised his sword, then addressed the neatly lined up troops.

"Sons of Ierilia. Today, we set out to wage the biggest battle Ierilia has not witnessed for many centuries. We will not only be fighting men, but this is a battle against a fallen god and a mighty sorcerer. You will be facing beasts that none of us have ever seen, warriors created by the use of magick and sorcery. You will not only use your arrows, swords, and spears, but the fleet weapons you have been issued as well. Some of the creatures we will face cannot be killed by a mere sword or a spear. With us is Cewrick, his son Icaras, Astiana, Taylith, Jonathan, and Ciara. Their powers and magick will assist us. May the gods and goddesses bless you all, keep you safe, and bring victory to us." Pointing his sword toward the troops, he shouted, "For Ierilia!"

"For Ierilia!" The men echoed his cry and held up their swords.

Brenn pulled on the reins and turned his horse. "The journey begins." He trotted ahead. The women were behind him, the men flanking the women, with Aldis bringing up the rear.

Taylith made sure he rode beside Laura. "Are you ready for this, love?"

"As ready as I'll ever be. I guess it'll be slow going since the troops are on foot."

"Yes. Scouts will ride ahead and report back if they see anything out of the ordinary."

They had ridden for several hours when two scouts came galloping toward them. Brenn held his hand up, halting them.

"General, Ticweapo has been attacked. Many of the men were taken, some killed. The women reported the attackers were half-man half beast and like giants."

"When did this happen?" Brenn asked.

"Just before we got there. We followed their tracks. Some led the other way, probably the ones with the prisoners, but the rest of the tracks point this way. The marauders are traveling through the forest, coming toward us."

"How many?"

"The women said there were at least a hundred or more."

"Pass this information down the lines and warn every warrior to be on the alert," Brenn ordered the captain of the first unit.

The scouts took off again and Brenn turned to face his team. "We may well be facing our first battle soon. Be prepared. Guard the king and the women." He motioned to carry on.

They continued for a while, but then heavy footfalls sounded from both sides. Within seconds, a horde of giant beasts attacked. They stood upright like humans, but they had two heads, one facing front, the other facing backward, and a large eye on each side of a grotesque face. They had a snout like a kora with large, protruding teeth. Their skin was green and reptilian. They needed no weapons. Their claws were the size of shovels, with talons just as long. Taylith remained in position to protect Laura. He winced as he saw warriors fly through the air, the snow staining red with blood. One of them lunged for him. He had his sword ready and swung it high, right at its throat. The sword glowed as it sliced the monster's head clean off its body.

But the body continued on, now groping and clawing blindly. Taylith pulled his fleet weapon from its holster and shot at it, the beam hardly injuring it.

"Use your swords. Pierce the heart!" Brenn shouted while fighting off a beast.

Taylith lunged for where the heart should be, but again, it made no difference as the blade pierced the giant chest. He wanted to shift. His dragon could slay these monstrosities easily, but he could not leave Laura unprotected.

Icaras, next to him, chanted and held his hand toward the monster. Green fire shot from his fingers, shattering the body into pieces. Chunks of green flesh fell to the ground. Taylith shuddered as one of its arms lay writhing in the snow, spilling yellow ooze from its ripped flesh.

The battle seemed to last forever, but when it was over and the last of the creatures retreated into the forest, it had really only lasted a short while.

He turned to Laura, who was leaning forward and hanging onto her horse's neck, her knuckles white as she gripped its mane. "It's over, love. You can sit up now."

"Headcount, please!" Brenn yelled. "How many did we lose? How many wounded?"

"Are you all right, Laura?" Taylith worried at her pale face.

"I'm okay." She gestured to the limb lying on the ground. "Is this what we're up against?"

Taylith nodded, his lips set in a grim line. "Yes, and probably worse."

One of the captains rode to the front. "General, three dead, two of them engineered warriors, and fifteen wounded."

"Thank you, Tanar. Jason, gather the other medics and please go and see to the wounded and report back to me? Captain Blunar, please see to the cremation of the dead?" He turned to the team. "We need to find shelter so we can rest and have lunch.

They waited for a report from Jason. He came back quite fast. "No serious injuries. I can tend to them when we rest, General."

Cewrick called out to Brenn. "When we find a suitable resting area, I can place a protection spell around it, so we can rest in peace."

"Good. Make it so."

They waited until the dead had been taken care of, then rode until they came to the base of the snow-laden mountains.

Brenn halted the troops. "We will stop and take respite here." He gestured to several of his men. "Scout the area. We need shelter for the wounded."

Moments later, the scouts returned. One of them stepped forward to report. "General, there is an outcropping of rocks just beyond that copse of trees. It should be large enough for the wounded men."

"Thank you, Lieutenant. Inform the medics to bring the wounded to the area."

They dismounted and led their horses through the copse of trees and found the outcropping of rocks.

Taylith quickly scanned the area. The trek through the mountains would be long and tedious. A thick blanket of snow covered the mountain pass and weighed down the branches of trees. The danger of an avalanche would be high once the men started the climb.

The mountain range was called Neverending Hills, the pass, Ogh Summit, the road through it created by centuries of merchants and their wagons filled with goods. Taylith wondered how they traveled through during the midst of winter. The snow looked undisturbed. Maybe they took a vacation during the snowfall season. *Ciara, we need to scout the area from above. The road through the mountain is covered in heavy snow.*

Ciara glanced at Taylith. *Brenn will not like it, but I agree. We can try to make a safe passage.*

Aldis called out to a couple of the men. "See to it the horses are fed and watered."

"Cewrick, shield the area." Brenn turned to Ciara. "Ciara, you and the women take shelter under the rocks with the wounded."

Taylith heard the low whisper of a chant as Cewrick cast his spell. "It is done. We should be safe here to rest."

Laura rubbed her legs vigorously, then blew on her hands. "Oh my God. I'm cold and stiff."

Taylith gazed down at her. Her face was no longer pale but flushed pink from the cold. "You are not used to riding." He caressed her cheek. "Do as Brenn said and go with Ciara. It will be safer and much warmer than out in the open."

For a moment he thought Laura would argue, but she clamped her mouth in a tight line and nodded, then followed Ciara, Erica, and Astiana to the shelter. One of the men had built a small fire under the outcropping, and Jason was already tending the wounded. The other three medics and the women joined in to assist him.

Satisfied that Laura would stay put, Taylith turned to the team. "Your Majesty, for your safety, I suggest you join the wounded under the shelter."

Biryn's eyes flashed. "I do not need to be coddled. I am just as skilled as the rest of you and can protect myself."

Taylith gave Biryn a hard look. "Your abilities are not in

question, but the protection of the crown is. Zohmes' spies have probably already reported that you have joined your troops. We cannot chance you being wounded, or worse, killed."

Brenn clapped Biryn on the shoulder. "He is right, Your Majesty. Let us not make a target of you while we rest."

Biryn took a deep breath and nodded, then made his way to the outcropping of rocks.

Aldis gestured to the mountain pass. "We need to try to figure out a way across this mountain. The trail is impassable."

Taylith glanced at the area where the road would normally be visible. "Ciara and I can scout the area. We can get a better view from the air. If the snow is not too heavy, we may be able to shift it to clear a path."

"I'd rather Ciara stay within the safety of Cewrick's shield," Brenn growled.

Ivran gave Taylith a curious look. "Shift it how?"

"We do not just breathe fire as dragons, and without the curse, Ciara has her full powers. She can use them in dragon form as well."

"As can you, Taylith." Ciara walked up to stand beside Brenn. "Between the two of us we can cut a path and create a barrier to offset an avalanche."

Brenn crossed his arms over his chest. "It is not safe for you to fly out on your own, princess. We are at war and I will not chance it."

"I am a guardian of Ierilia... A dragon...and a sorceress. I can take care of myself, Brenn. I have done so for centuries." Ciara clasped Brenn's hand.

Taylith knew exactly how Brenn felt. It still unsettled him that he had to bring Laura with them. "She will not be flying alone, Brenn. I will allow no harm to come to her." He glanced at Ciara. *Do not be too rough on him, Ciara. He worries for you as I do for Laura.*

He heard Ciara's chuckle in his mind. *Not too long ago you were much harder on him when you thought he had put my life in danger.*

Taylith knew he was hard on Brenn. The cousin he had given his freedom to save had come close to killing herself. When the team had been trapped by a horde of Zohmes' giant rat-creatures, on their search for Cylena, Ciara and Icaras had depleted their powers to exhaustion to keep the monsters at bay. If Rania had not sent Taylith to intervene, all of them would have perished. *I will not allow you to take unnecessary risks.*

"We have no other choice. The road is impassable. We risk the lives of all if we try to march the men through the pass," Aldis remarked.

"Come, Ciara, we must find an open space to shift." Taylith took her hand, but before they had a chance to leave the group, Jonathan ran past them, left the protected area, and headed toward the pass.

"What is he doing?" Laura shouted. "Jonathan, come back!"

Taylith stood rooted as he watched Jonathan begin to spin, his body whirling faster and faster until he was nothing but a blurry myriad of colors. Chanting drifted toward them, loud, then booming, as the vortex that had been Jonathan moved toward the pass.

The snow shifted, crawled slowly up the sides of the mountain, and stuck there as if held by glue. Awed, Taylith watched the whirlwind disappear from sight. Before their eyes, a clear path appeared through the mountain ridge. "It appears Jonathan solved our problem."

Laura came running toward them and stopped beside

Taylith. "My God. My nephew the super wizard. It scares me, Taylith. Is he more Zohmes than Julia?"

The swirling mass of color came back toward them, the plasma slowly fading as Jonathan came closer to the protective shield, until he was again himself.

"I don't know how I did that," he muttered as he joined the team.

Ciara patted him on the back. "Good work, Jonathan. Think back to before you ran from us. What were you thinking about?"

"I was listening to the argument whether you two should shift to your dragons when I imagined a large rotor clearing a path for us. Next I knew, my feet acted on their own."

"You are the true son of a god. Your Earth DNA has not affected your powers," Astiana said.

"I told you before. I don't want to be known as the son of that bastard."

Astiana sighed. "Unfortunately, it is what it is. You are directly descended from a god and have inherited all his godly powers and the magick of your forefathers."

The others praised Jonathan, but he merely scowled. "It scares the shit out of me."

Taylith sat on a stone and pulled Laura down to sit on his lap. "As long as you use it for the good of all men and women, and the planet, there is nothing to fear. I, for one, would like to eat and drink before we continue."

The others agreed. They would have to eat quickly and start their trek up the mountain if they wished to reach the other side of the ridge by nightfall.

Brenn called out to Jason. "How are the repairs to our men coming along?"

"Mostly done, General. I have replaced spare parts, screws, bolts, and nuts and welded together what was split. I also did an oil and grease change, added fuel, and — "

Brenn grimaced while Erica and Laura burst into laughter. "Enough. I get the point. Bad choice of words. I gather you are telling me you have finished tending to the wounded. Good. We will take a short break to eat before we proceed."

CHAPTER SEVENTEEN

The path Jonathan had created was wide enough for two. It was going to take some time before all the troops made it through. Laura rode close to Taylith, all the while glancing up at the shorn off walls of snow beside them. She had never been to the mountains on Earth, but she knew avalanches could happen with a sneeze. Had Jonathan secured the heavy snow enough so that it wouldn't fall and bury them?

She shifted in her saddle and grimaced. "It feels as if we've been riding for hours."

Taylith looked at her, his face filled with concern. "Are you keeping warm enough?"

She nodded. "Yes, the skin suit keeps me toasty warm and the gloves help." She knew he was worried about her, that he didn't really want her with them. They had no idea how long this war would last, and there was no way in hell she could stay behind while the man she loved risked his life. If something were to happen to Taylith, she couldn't bear it. The thought of this war scared the hell out of her. And that horde of creatures that had attacked them was horrendous. Neither Taylith's sword nor his fleet weapon had affected the monster he fought. It just kept coming even without a head. How did they fight a war against creatures like that? She took a deep breath and shook the thoughts from her mind. "How much farther before we make camp?"

"From what I know, it will probably take us until nightfall to reach the other side of these mountains. There is a vast forest on the other side we must travel through before we reach the next mountain ridge."

Night fell fast in and just beyond the mountains. It was already dark when Taylith helped Laura from her horse and tied the reins to a tree at the edge of the thick forest.

"We will camp here for the night. Stay close together." Brenn marched along the edge of the forest to speak to his warriors. "Set your tents up next to each other."

Taylith leaned down and kissed her cheek before joining the men to set up the tent for the team. There were no solitary tents on this mission. Each troop had their own tent that the warriors shared, and the team had one they had to share.

While the men set up the tent, the women gathered firewood. By the time they were finished with the tent, a large crackling fire burned.

Cewrick had created another shield along the edge of the forest and behind the tents. The women sat close to the fire, all enjoying the heat radiating from the flames.

Taylith joined Laura and warmed his hands near the fire. "I am going to see if I can find us something to roast. Warm food would be very welcome right now. Anyone want to go with me?"

"I will." Laura began to stand.

"No. Leave the men to do the hunting. Jonathan, join me?" They headed into the forest, their initiative followed by the other men.

Laura sat back down, frustrated that Taylith insisted she

stay behind. She was really getting tired of being treated as a child, and she was surprised Erica would put up with the medieval attitudes from the men. "Are the guys always like this on missions? We aren't children."

"No, they are not." Erica sighed. "You pick your battles... This isn't one of them." She grinned at Laura. "And you, honey, married a dragon. Did you expect he'd change the protective attitude once the ceremony happened?"

Astiana glanced at her. "This is not just any mission, Laura. This is war. One we will not win if we do not follow the orders of those who are experienced."

Laura threw a twig into the fire. "But this was only to hunt. What would it hurt to let one of us go with them?"

Ciara twisted a lock of her raven hair around her finger. "Cewrick has shielded the camp from Zohmes' minions. Taylith would never risk your life by allowing you to breach its safety."

Laura clenched her jaw. "But he will risk his and I am supposed to just step back and let him do it?"

"Taylith is a dragon and a very powerful sorcerer. Even if he were not, I Am protects him... But you are human and can be very easily broken." Ciara clasped Laura's hands. *Do not forget he has seen you close to death and will never forgive himself for the role his black dragon played in your captivity and torture.*

It was not his fault! Laura looked at Ciara in surprise. "Brenn is human...well, a lion, too... You don't fear for his life?"

Ciara smiled. "Taylith will ensure that Brenn returns to me in one piece." *Nevertheless, Taylith holds himself responsible. His soul was bound to yours even as a black dragon, and as your lifemate, he is your guardian and protector. Do not make it harder for him to see to your safety.*

Laura winced and nodded. Had she been making it harder for Taylith? She had fought Julia tooth and nail when she thought her sister was treating her like a child. It became much worse after the crash and her captivity. At least until John had come in the picture. Even Mark had coddled her. And she had allowed it. She was a mere shell of her former self until Taylith had come into the picture. It had aggravated the hell out of her when he was first assigned to guard her and the others. He insisted she be escorted whenever she left the estate. Thinking back, she realized he also treated Tomas, Kira, and Reana in the same manner.

Erica slapped her cheek. "Mosquitos? In this weather?"

"What is that?" Ciara asked.

"Small bugs that bite. I thought I felt one crawling on my cheek."

Laura rubbed her face. "I thought I felt something, too."

Astiana held out a hand. A small, winged bug landed on top of her fingers. "It is quite friendly. Looking at it closely, it is quite beautiful. Almost a miniature dragon. Look at its tail."

The other three leaned close to look at the creature.

"Geez, I hope I didn't kill the one I swiped at," Laura said. "I wish the guys would return. They have been gone a long time."

The men came back carrying the game they had caught and skinned. With the cold weather and snow, Taylith was surprised that they had managed to catch enough game for both dinner and breakfast the next morning. There was enough for all of them, and even for some of the warriors.

"Taylith, look at this little bug. It is friendly and seems to like us." It flew down to sit on Laura's hand. She held out her hand, the tiny little insect resting on her finger.

Taylith handed his catch to Brenn, who threaded a stick through it and held it over the fire along with his own catch. "See if it will come to me."

Laura held her hand close to Taylith's and the little bug jumped onto his.

Taylith held a glimmer stick close to the creature. "It is a very tiny jewel dragon. Unbelievable. I have never heard of such."

"How could it have survived in this intense cold?" Laura wondered.

Taylith noticed Ciara get up and start to walk away. "Ciara, do not leave camp. We did not see anything while we hunted for food, but there could be some of Zohmes' minions lurking in the forest."

"I need some quiet time. I will be back in a minute."

"Maybe she needs to go to the loo," Laura told Taylith.

"Loo?"

"Relieve herself."

Taylith shrugged. "As long as she does not leave the protection of Cewrick's shield."

Ciara did not take long. "I spoke with Rania. The miniature dragon is a jewel dragon bespelled by Odoxon centuries ago, when he was much younger. We can undo the spell, but she must drink from the enchanted waters of the glitter basin. It is a pond that is hidden in the Jagirra Grotto. The grotto is somewhere within the next mountain ridge beyond the forest, the Vlolf Mountains."

"That means she will need to come with us. Do you think she understands us?" Taylith examined the little dragon. She was a perfectly formed miniature, all the way down to her delicate wings and long, gleaming tail. Her minuscule scales glittered gold in the firelight.

Ciara carefully took the dragon and held her close to her

face. She whispered a few words, then nodded. "She cannot speak, but she knows we will help her and will fly with us."

Taylith watched the little dragon fly up to perch on a branch above them, then curl up to rest. *Ciara, I do not recognize her dragon. Do you know who she could be?*

I don't know. Rania said she was bespelled centuries ago. It had to be before the curse and long before we were born.

"I wonder if there are any more." Jonathan poked a stick in the coals of the fire.

Ciara shook her head. "I do not think so. Rania did not mention any others."

Erica leaned up against Laro, her head resting on his shoulder. "Why would Doxie put a spell on just one jewel dragon?"

"You are as clueless as I am. I can only share what Rania has told me," Ciara stated.

"We will be traveling that route anyway. We can deviate long enough to free her from the spell," Biryn stated.

"This is all we need. A mission within a mission," Laura complained. "But I guess we have to help the little critter."

"Food is ready," Brenn announced.

"I'm so hungry I'll eat anything right now," Erica muttered.

"Even roasted kurakelda?" Laro cast Erica a sidelong glance.

Erica scrunched up her nose. "Eeewww! No! I'd never be hungry enough to eat one of those."

Laura glanced at Erica. "What's a kurakelda?"

Erica shuddered. "A nasty, gigantic fucking spider."

Laura screwed up her face. "Oh yuck! No way! You guys eat spiders?"

Taylith laughed. It was good they could still find humor in this serious situation. "I have never eaten kurakelda. Do not worry, we found some birds and an onnagus. All are meats you have eaten at home."

They ate and drank some water, then passed around a wineskin. The sounds of the warriors around them began to quieten as they retired to their tents.

Taylith yawned. Fatigue had set in, especially after he had filled his stomach. He caressed Laura's leg. "I think I am going to the tent. Brenn said we leave at first light."

She nodded. "I'm right with you. I just need to go to the back of the tent for a few minutes."

He had already crawled into their sleeping bag when she joined him. "Feel better now?"

She wriggled into the sleeping bag and snuggled up against him. "Yes. Looks like everyone is crashing for the night. I wish we had our own tent."

"Sweetness, we could never carry that much equipment for everyone to have their own private tent. We have to make do."

"Well, damn, we're newly married and we can't even—"

"Who says we cannot?"

"We're sleeping in our clothes, and—"

"Hush, woman. Honestly, do you have that on your mind all the time? Be happy we can be in each other's arms. Maybe when everyone is asleep we can—"

"Yeah, like hell. I'm not having sex with everyone around us."

Taylith chuckled, took her into his arms, and kissed her. "Then sleep, my sweet lady. Just be happy we are together."

CHAPTER EIGHTEEN

Taylith woke to the murmur of the troops as they readied themselves and took down their tents. The smell of roasting meat filled the air, and a quick scan of the tent showed him the others were already up.

He gently shook Laura's shoulder. "Laura, time to wake up."

She looked at him groggily. "Already? Every muscle and bone in my body aches like all bloody hell."

He tugged the sleeping bag from her. "Hurry. We don't want to keep them waiting."

She yanked the covers from his hand. "You're so mean."

Taylith brushed his fingers across her cheek. "Sweetness, this is what war is all about. We sleep early, and we get up at first light to continue. Better get used to it. It will be a couple of months before we meet up with Zohmes' real army. And the gods only know what we will encounter before that."

Laura stood and stretched. "Don't we have to find that grotto today?"

"Yes, if we can get through the forest fast enough. It is quite a trek to the next mountain ridge."

She stood on her tiptoes and gave him a quick kiss. "I'll be with you shortly. I need to visit the little girl's room first."

Taylith gave her a confused look. "Little girl's room?"

"Dammit. Why do I have to explain it all the time? I need to go pee!" She grumbled as she stepped out of the tent.

Taylith packed up their bedroll and shook his head. *If you do not want me to ask, then use phrases I understand.* He heard her soft reply in his mind.

I'm being a real pain in the ass, aren't I?

Yes, she was, but he was smart enough not to verbally agree with her or even think it. It would only make matters worse.

He had just finished packing their supplies and left the tent to join the others when Laura walked up beside him and grabbed his arm, stopping him.

She slipped her arms around his waist and hugged him. "I love you, Taylith. I'm sorry that I'm being such a jerk about everything." She rested her head against his shoulder and mumbled against his chest, "I *can* take care of myself even if you may not think so."

"Your ability to take care of yourself has never been in question." He sighed and kissed the top of her head, then held her. She was no longer the traumatized woman he had first seen after her captivity, and he would do nothing to squash her fight to find her place in this new life. He understood her battle. She had not been much older than him when the dragons were captured. Because of their recklessness, before the curse, Ciara's father had often made the threat to bind his and Ciara's ability to fly. He was surprised his uncle had not done so.

"I love you, too, sweetness." When he finally released her, he gazed down into those sparkling green eyes. "We should join the others."

She nodded, then gave him a quizzical look. "Ciara has the power to heal and you helped me and Mark. What did you see that changed your mind about me coming with you?"

He clenched his jaw. "We will need more than just Ciara and I to make a difference in this war." He clamped his lips together. A path had been written in the book of knowledge. To deviate from it could alter the outcome. If he shared what he had seen about her or the team, their first course of action would be to try to keep Ivran safe from harm. That very act could alter the outcome. He was not about to leave Reana without her lifemate and little Issa without a father...or lose another friend to Zohmes. He had to let the vision play out as written.

"That's it?"

"That is all I can tell you." He took her hand and led her to the fire and joined the team.

"Morning. Most of us have eaten already," Erica told them. "I kept some meat aside for you both, though."

"Thank you, Erica." Taylith smiled gratefully. Roasted meat was preferable over the dry rations. He took the stick from her and munched on the meat. To his surprise, the tiny dragon landed on his knee and sat there. It was almost as if she was watching him.

"You've made a little friend." Laura held her hand out to the bug, but it stayed on Taylith's leg.

"Maybe she senses that Ciara and I are dragons."

They ate, drank their water ration, and Taylith got up to help the men dismantle the tent and pack their gear on their two pack horses. When they were finished, Brenn faced the troops that were already lined up and waiting.

"Men, this forest is dense. You need eyes front, back, and both sides. Danger could lurk anywhere, even from above. Be on the alert at all times."

Aldis took a horn from his belt and sounded it, alerting the troops that they were ready to advance into the forest. Aldis and Brenn led, with warriors flanking the team on both sides and behind.

Taylith rode behind Aldis and Brenn, Laura beside him. The little dragon had planted herself between his horse's ears.

Biryn, behind them, complained. "I should be leading my army instead of warriors coddling me."

Taylith turned his head. "Your Majesty, you have a general to lead your army. We cannot allow any harm to befall you. You must be guarded at all times."

"So Brenn is allowed to get hurt or worse, killed?"

"That is his job." Taylith would do everything in his power to protect Brenn from harm. If something were to happen to Ciara's lifemate, it would destroy her, and that he would never permit.

They rode in silence for a few hours, the only sounds the murmurs of the warriors, their marching feet, and the horses snorting occasionally. The forest was silent, most animals hibernating for the winter. The birds had escaped to a warmer climate.

"Look, your little friend is flying away." Laura pointed to the little dragon as it fluttered ahead of them.

The sky was clear that day, the suns sending their rays through the branches of the trees. Taylith drew in his breath as a ray of sunlight lit up the tiny dragon and turned her into a gold jewel. She was beautiful beyond words. He wondered why she had flown away suddenly.

He did not have to wonder for too long. She came back and flew before his face, her wings flapping in an agitated manner. "I think our little friend is trying to tell us something. Danger up ahead?" he called out to Brenn and Aldis.

Aldis sounded the horn and held up his hand. The troops stopped. "I will pass it along the lines." Aldis rode to talk to the captain of the first troop to tell him to be on high alert and pass the message down to the others.

"I do not know what is up ahead. I wish your little friend could talk and tell us," Brenn told Taylith.

"Yes. So do I."

Aldis sounded the horn to proceed. They continued on, wary of any strange sound or suspicious shadows among the dense trees. Occasionally, a dump of snow from a tree would startle a horse and set the scouts scurrying into the forest to look for predators.

His little dragon sat between his horse's ears again. Taylith looked at Laura beside him. "Be careful, sweetness. Something is about to happen. I feel it."

A terrified scream came from somewhere behind them. Taylith swiveled his horse to see where it came from, but he hardly had time. Creatures attacked from the trees above. Green, almost the same color as the evergreen foliage of the trees, they would have been difficult to spot. They were the size of a man. Their heads were that of a reptile, their bodies covered in green scales. They had claws with two digits, long spikes protruding from each. Their eyes glowed orange. A long, forked tongue protruded from their maws. A thick, long tail extended from their back. They swished it around, sending warriors flying into the forest. There were hundreds of the reptiles falling from the branches to attack the troops. Thankfully, the fleet weapons were able to annihilate them. Nevertheless, they managed to harm some warriors.

Taylith yelled at Laura. "There's one behind you!" While he fought one off and shot it, from the corner of his eyes he saw Laura shoot her attacker, her other arm wielding her sword and managing to slice off the head of another. At the same time, another fell on him. Too late to draw his fleet weapon. He used his sword and sliced off its head. He realized he had to let Laura fight her own battle, that his lack of attention, even for a second, could have cost him dearly. He fought on, praying silently that the gods and goddesses would watch over Laura and the others.

The battle was finally over. Dead reptilian bodies and their body parts lay scattered on the ground, yellow slime oozing from the corpses staining the snow. Taylith had no idea if they had killed all the monsters or if the remainder had retreated. "Is anyone hurt?" he called out.

The team appeared to be fine. He got off his horse and walked along the troop lines with Brenn. "By the gods, the monsters Odoxon and Zohmes have created. When we face their army, what will we have to deal with?"

Brenn shrugged. "Probably no worse than this, except thousands more. They are trying very hard to stop us before we get that far."

"The little dragon tried to warn us."

One of the captains rode up to Brenn. "General, we have five wounded, though not seriously, and two were killed."

"We will ride ahead a short distance to get away from this carnage and stop for lunch, tend the wounded, see to the dead, and then continue," Brenn announced.

They continued until they found a small clearing away from the gore. The troops stopped on Brenn's signal and began caring for the wounded.

"I guess we get rations for lunch?" Laura dismounted and handed the reins of her horse to Taylith.

"Unless you want to eat roasted reptile?" Taylith secured their horses, then pulled a couple of packages of rations from his saddle bag and gave one to Laura.

She scrunched up her face. "You're joking, right?"

"Yes. Sorry. We do not have time to hunt for meat. Rations are our only choice."

"I don't mind the jerky. It's quite tasty, but kind of tough.

Something warm would be preferable in this weather, though." Laura pulled off a piece of the smoked meat with her teeth.

"We would be lucky to find any game now anyway. The closer we get to the mountains, the colder it gets." Taylith handed her the waterskin. The dragon fluttered around them to finally rest on his shoulder.

Laura gazed at the little dragon. "Should I be jealous? I wonder what she'll look like when the spell is lifted."

"You and I are mated. She hears and understands everything we say, so she knows I am unavailable."

"Why doesn't she go to Ciara? She's a dragon, too. It's weird."

Taylith looked at the dragon curled on his shoulder. "Maybe she feels safer with a man."

"She's survived for how many centuries on her own? I don't think that's the reason." She shook her head. "Never mind. As long as she doesn't become your pet once she's a human again. Looks like we're getting ready to move on."

Taylith waited for Laura to mount her horse, then got onto his. Aldis blew his horn and the trek to the grotto continued, with the tiny dragon leading the way now, flying ahead of Brenn and Aldis.

CHAPTER NINETEEN

They finally arrived at the base of the Vlolf Mountains. Like the last mountain ridge, the much steeper peaks were laden with snow.

Taylith looked to see if Jonathan was getting ready to clear a path for them, but instead, Cewrick and Icaras stepped forward. They chanted, holding out their hands in the direction where the little dragon hovered high above. Fire streamed from their hands. The snow melted, clearing a path for them.

"We will ride ahead and continue to clear the way," Cewrick told Brenn and Aldis.

"I wonder how far it is to the grotto," Taylith said.

"What do we do once we get there?" Laura wondered. "It involves only the team, not the few thousand warriors following us."

"They will have to wait, take a break while we do what we need to. Sending them on ahead would not be a good plan. They need Brenn's leadership."

Trudging through the muck and water was not easy going and slowed them down considerably. Horses slipped several times, almost falling. The warriors often waded through the mess up to their knees.

"Not a good place to take a break," Laura commented while pointing at the slush and water below her horse.

"It cannot be helped. Thousands of men will not fit inside that grotto."

They had plodded on for several hours when they came upon a cliff protruding from the side of the mountain. It protected the path, and quite a long section was clear of snow. When they were about halfway through, the little dragon became agitated and kept flying toward a narrow precipice resembling a jagged scar on the rock face.

"I think we have found the grotto!" Taylith called out to Brenn and Aldis.

Aldis sounded his horn and everyone stopped. "A good spot for the troops to take a break. Now where is it?"

Brenn dismounted and walked up to the opening. "Barely wide enough for a man to fit through. Does the whole team need to go, Ciara?"

"The four swords and those with magick. The others can stay here and rest," Ciara told them.

"No way. I'm going with Taylith," Laura exclaimed.

"And I am not allowing you to go in there unprotected. Who knows what is lurking in that grotto," Brenn told Ciara.

"You heard me. The four swords must go. I believe you have one?"

Brenn grunted. "Glimmer sticks ready? I will go in first."

One by one they edged through the opening. Once inside, they activated their glimmer sticks and looked at their surroundings.

Taylith edged closer to Laura. "Stay by my side. This is a perfect shelter for wild animals to hibernate."

The sticks lit up a medium-size grotto. Jagged rocks dotted the ground. Water ran down the walls steadily, forming a narrow stream at the bottom. At the far end was an opening to what looked like a tunnel. The grotto appeared empty.

The dragon led them to the tunnel entrance. It was just wide enough to walk single file, in some places so narrow, they had to squeeze through sideways. It suddenly ended and led into another grotto, smaller than the first one. Taylith noticed this one had no openings. Rocks were scattered on the ground, some as large as a man.

The dragon flew to a huge flat rock and sat on top of it, her wings flapping.

Taylith laid his hand on the rock. "I think this is covering up an entrance."

"And how are we supposed to move that thing?" Laura asked. "It's more than a foot thick."

Their voices echoed through the grotto. Ciara stepped forward, placed her hand on the rock, then turned to face the team. "The four swords. Touch the top, bottom, and each side with the point of the blade."

Brenn, Erica, Taylith, and Biryn drew their swords. When all four tips touched the stone face firmly, the rock began to move to the side until it revealed a perfectly hewn entrance. Brilliant light blinded them for a moment, causing them to shield their eyes.

Once their eyes adjusted to the brightness, they stepped through the opening.

"Oh my God! It's fucking gorgeous!" Erica wandered further into what looked like an ancient temple within a large cavern.

Taylith walked around slowly examining the etchings on the walls. "I bet these tell a story."

Hundreds of crystals in a myriad of colors dotted the walls. In the center of the cave stood an altar, on top of it, two gold candlesticks and an ancient book covered in gold.

At the base of the altar was a large round basin filled with glittering water. Small golden sparkles floated above it.

"It's magical," Taylith whispered. "It must have been created by the gods and goddesses."

"I wonder what's in the book." Jonathan tried to move behind the altar, but an invisible shield blocked him.

"The book is protected by the gods." Astiana approached the altar and tentatively reached for the book, her hand breaching the shield.

Suddenly the book flipped open and pages began to turn, then stopped as quickly as it had started. She took the book in her hands and gestured to the open page. "I have opened the shield. Come, join hands. We must work this spell when the dragon drinks from the water."

Ciara, Cewrick, Biryn, Taylith, Jonathan, and Icaras joined Astiana. Standing around the altar, hands linked, Astiana read the spell to them first. Then they began chanting it together.

From the corner of his eyes, Taylith saw the little dragon fly to the glittering water and lower her head to drink. A golden light surrounded her tiny body, growing larger as the chant grew in crescendo. Sparks flashed, the glow so bright he had to shield his eyes, then dissipating in a brilliant shower of sparkles. When the light faded, a woman kneeled before the shimmering pool, head bowed, her raven hair spilling over her shoulders and covering her face.

The woman stood, her body clad in leathers as if she were a warrior ready for battle. She raised her head, brushing her hair out of her face. "I am Liana, daughter of King Jelano and Queen Copera of Storming Enclave."

The chanting stopped. Taylith stared at the young woman as if she were an alien from outer space. He stepped away from the altar, took a few steps toward Liana, and halted.

"Impossible," he muttered.

Liana came toward him. He took a step back, hardly believing what his eyes saw. The young woman could be Ciara's sister. The likeness was unbelievable. She claimed to be the daughter of his parents? He had never had a sister. Would his father and mother not have told him about her? He turned to face the others. "This is a trick. It has to be an Odoxon or Zohmes hallucination. I do not and never have had a sister."

Ciara and Astiana approached him. "Calm down, Taylith," Astiana told him while patting his arm. "Let the young woman talk."

His heart pounded so hard, he could hear it echo in his ears. A sister? Impossible. Then again, his parents had been mated for centuries before Taylith came along. But why would they have hidden that they had had another child? A child that had obviously disappeared?

Liana held her hands out to him. "Taylith, you are my brother. You look so much like Mother but with Father's coloring, like me, I suppose..." She sighed and lowered her hands. "I was born many centuries ago and had a very happy childhood. My...or...our parents loved me dearly and I was my father's princess. Then I grew up into a young woman. Odoxon was a much younger man then. Or...I should say, sorcerer. He pursued me, wanted me for his mate. I refused his advances and had no interest in him. I knew we were not lifemates. My soul shard could never be shared with him. Besides that, I had no feelings for the man.

"Yet he continued to hound me and would not give up. I was a rebellious daughter — I often shifted to my dragon and flew to forbidden regions. My...our...parents worried for me. I frequently got into trouble, and our father would punish me and bind me to my quarters.

179

"One day, when I was free to roam, I shifted to my dragon and flew to this region, seeking this temple I had learned about, determined to find it. Odoxon had kept watch on my movements. When I arrived in the grotto, he was there. He demanded I accept him as a mate. I refused and was about to leave this place when he placed the shrinking spell on me and bound me to the grotto, mountains, and the forest, forever, until I would agree to be his mate."

Taylith found his voice, although it came out rather croaky. "Why did Father and Mother not tell me about you? Why was your disappearance kept such a secret? Surely Ciara's parents would have known you?"

"I cannot answer those questions. You will have to speak to our parents and our family. I am sure my disappearance will have caused much pain."

Ciara approached Liana and held out her hand. "So we are cousins. You should be so much older than us, yet here you are, still a young woman. What do I say? You look so much like me, you could be my sister. I have always longed to have a sister or brother. Welcome, Liana."

Tears soaked Liana's cheeks as she pulled Ciara into an embrace.

Seeing the two together warmed the cockles of Taylith's heart. He had to believe this was true. This was not a Zohmes or Odoxon trick. He joined the two women and pulled them both into his arms.

Brenn interrupted the emotional trio. "I hate to disturb the three of you, but we have a war to fight. The question is now, Liana, do you remember how to get home?"

The three broke apart, Liana stepping toward Brenn. Taylith watched her dapper stature. Short, like Ciara, she appeared brave and determined.

"General, I have no wish to go home. I know my parents

will be overjoyed at my return, to learn that I did not die, but that will have to wait. Please do not send word back about this. I will go with you. I have all my powers again and am as skilled, if not more, than Ciara. My anger at Odoxon and what he subjected me to for all these centuries, and all the time I have lost, boils within me like a festering wound. I want my revenge!"

Taylith held his breath to see what Brenn would respond, until Astiana spoke.

"Rania just spoke to me. Liana must go with us. She will be a great aid in the approaching war."

"When we leave this temple, the rock will seal it again. It belongs to the goddess of light, Urena," Liana told them.

"So many gods and goddesses," Erica murmured. "I find it hard to remember all their names."

"And you could not enter the temple ever?" Jonathan asked Liana.

"No. The seal was too tight. Also, without the removal of the spell, it would have done me no good. I am thankful the book of knowledge decreed I should finally be freed."

Taylith joined Laura and grasped her hand. "She is my sister."

"I heard. And I saw. She could be Ciara's sister. The likeness is uncanny."

"I am still overwhelmed by it all." He squeezed her hand, grateful of her understanding.

"I bet. It is a lot to take in. Your parents are the ones that are going to be shocked out of their minds."

"Yes. She should be going home. But you heard Astiana."

A murmur sounded and echoed from the troops when they came out of the grotto and joined the team members left behind. Taylith could hardly resent the gossip. They had gone into the grotto with a tiny bug, although the troops did not know about her. And they came out with a look-alike Ciara.

"What do we tell the men?" Brenn looked at them inquiringly.

"We rescued a princess. What else can we tell them?" Ciara answered.

"It is near nightfall. We may as well camp here for the night," Aldis suggested.

Cewrick put up a shield to protect them from the intense cold. The men searched for wood to build fires, and since there was no room to put up the tents, they placed their bedrolls close to the fire.

Sitting around the fire, munching on dried smoked meat, Liana told her story again. After she finished talking, she turned to Laura. "You are my sister now. You have brought my brother much happiness. I hope we will be close."

"Honestly, I was a little jealous of you. Afraid of your human coveting my man. But now? I am overwhelmed by all of it. Your father and mother are going to die when they see you after so long. Wrong word choice. They will surely faint or something. Do you know I'm from another planet?"

"Yes. You are from Earth. But you were destined to be my brother's mate. It was written. Just like my destiny was written. I am so overjoyed to be back, to be myself again. I truly hope we can be sisters."

Taylith felt Laura snuggle against him. "I think I'm going to love that little sister of yours."

"Little? You do realize she is much older than me?"

Laura giggled. "Just by a few centuries."

They finally bedded down for the night, the events in the temple haunting Taylith's dreams.

Dawn had barely shown its nose when they woke up. The fire was still smoldering. To Taylith's surprise, Ivran had caught a korobeast and was roasting the meat over the glowing embers. They would have meat to last a couple of days.

"Looks like the troops are almost ready to move on," he commented.

"Yes. Soon as we have eaten, we will." Brenn gave his horse some oats and put his bedroll on the packhorse.

One of the captains approached them leading a sable stallion, then handed the reins to Brenn. "Please, take my horse for the princess to ride. I will march with my men."

Brenn tied the reins to a tree with the team's horses. "Thank you, Captain Ryston. He will be well cared for."

Taylith thanked the captain, too. The captain bowed his head, then left to join his men. The man was one of the genetically engineered warriors and led a legion of them. At least half of the army was made up of these men.

Taylith smiled at Liana. She appeared to be well rested and in good spirits. "Liana, you slept well?"

"Thank you, brother. Yes. I felt safe for the first time in centuries."

Taylith still found it hard to believe she was his sister. That he even had a sister. One that was supposed to be so much older than him, yet she seemed younger right now. He was glad that like Ciara, she had been spared being cursed as a black dragon, although living as a miniature bound to the forest and the grotto was just as bad. How were his parents going to react upon their return? Why did she have to go along with them? Were they really going to defeat Odoxon? And Zohmes? The questions troubled his mind. He shook his head to clear it. "Let us enjoy some of this warm food. Who knows when we have a chance to catch any more." He handed a stick with meat to Laura and Liana.

CHAPTER TWENTY

They had traveled for weeks. The Vlolf mountain range was vast. It was going to take them a long time to cross them. The weather was slowly changing from severe winter to the beginning of spring. The snow was melting. Wildlife emerged from their hibernation, so they were able to catch enough game for their meals.

"This is the last ridge we need to cross," Brenn announced while they rested for lunch.

"Still a lot of snow to deal with," Taylith said.

"Yes, and thaw has set in. Not good." Erica munched on her meat.

"Why, Erica?" Ivran asked.

"Avalanches. I learned a lot about them on Earth. A whole bunch of snow can let loose and suddenly fall and bury a whole village. Or in this case, all of us. Even a sudden loud noise can cause an avalanche."

"Yes, we have had such happen before. The troops have already been warned," Brenn said.

"Let's hope they heed the warning," Laura told them.

Taylith looked at Liana. "Are you sorry you decided to go with us?"

Liana raised her chin, sparks of light flashing in her violet eyes, the pupils that of her dragon. "No. I am determined to pay Odoxon back for what he has done to me and our parents."

Taylith cast her a sidelong glance. "You do realize he is a powerful old sorcerer?"

"Yes, I know, brother. So am I. Between us, we should be able to get rid of him. There is a lot of magick in this group."

"Believe me, we have tried. I truly hope we can best Odoxon and Zohmes in this war. I am surprised Odoxon did not strip you of your magick. Many of us had to go to the Clyss for our powers to be restored."

"He did not strip me of my magick, but while I was so small, I could not use them. They were there, but dormant. I am ready to do battle with that old man."

Jonathan stepped beside Liana. "We will hand their asses back to them. There is no bloody way I am returning home until we send the twisted bastards packing."

Taylith prayed to the gods that that were the case. The vision he was given had warned him of the war, but he was not shown the outcome.

They finished eating, packed their supplies, and quickly mounted their horses. Taylith urged his horse on to ride alongside Laura. The pass was large enough for at least three to ride side by side, but the trek over the ridge would be tedious. The path was now a thick layer of mud covered by slick ice and splotches of snow. They had to urge the horses on slowly to avoid their hooves from sliding in the mud. The further they ascended the ridge, the more restless the men became. The snow and ice was thickening due to the colder air closer to the peak.

A sick feeling settled in the pit of Taylith's stomach, setting him on edge. He scanned the forest and the trees. With the snow thawing and the sounds of animals and birds in the forest around them, it was easier for Zohmes' creatures to hide in wait.

A shot fired, echoing through the trees. Moments later, the ground shook, causing their horses to shift restlessly. The sound of trees snapping echoed through the mountains, and a loud rumbling noise resounded from above. Plumes of snow and ice rose in the air above them, a massive snowpack tumbling fast down the side of the ridge and moving straight at them.

"Avalanche!" one of the warriors yelled behind them.

Taylith knew they would have to act fast or they would lose the whole army to the wall of ice. *Ciara, Liana...We need to shift and redirect the ice.*

Cewrick's chanting voice sounded above the loud crashing of the snow slide. Icaras, Astiana, Jonathan, and Biryn joined in the chant. Taylith had to trust them to keep the team and as many of the men as they could safe within a shield. He leaped from his horse, moving far enough away to shift, Ciara and Liana doing the same.

The dragons took to the air. From above, Taylith could see the barrage of snow picking up speed. Screams rent the air. Some of the troops scattered, running away from the wall of ice barreling toward them, but the shield held steady against the torrent. He took a deep, rumbling breath, blowing hard at the hundreds of tons of ice and snow, forcing it away from the men on the ground. Ciara and Liana followed his lead. Using their powers, they drove the mass of rocks, broken trees, ice, and snow away from the mountain pass and the troops in its path.

The dragons flew above the carnage. Taylith's heart sank as he took in the sight below. A wide path of destruction had cut through the forest, taking trees, rocks, and any animal along with it. Much of the mountain pass was covered in a sheet of icy debris. He knew there was no possible way they had saved everyone, but a quick glance at the head of the pass showed him the team and the king were safe. *We need to split up and search for survivors.*

They spread out and scanned the area. It was no telling how far the river of snow and ice had taken its victims. A couple of miles down the pass, Taylith spotted movement. Several of the men had pulled themselves from the debris and were crouched down, digging in the snow and ice with their hands. Another group of warriors had left the safety of the unmarred trees to assist them. *There, do you see them?*

I do. Liana, stay with Taylith. I will return with Cewrick, Jonathan, and Icaras. They can assist us in removing the snow. Ciara turned and flew back to the team.

After Ciara had returned with the three men, she assisted them on the ground, using magick to help hold the snow away from any wounded they found. Liana and Taylith carefully shifted the snow and debris in layers to keep it from collapsing and killing anyone that may be trapped beneath it. By the time they were finished working their way through the ice and snow, Taylith had counted two hundred and fifty-two men that had lost their lives and over sixty wounded. At least half of those men hung onto life by a mere thread.

Taylith and Liana landed in a clearing and shifted back to their humans. More of the army had found their way to the cleared area. They made their way to Ciara and the others.

Liana studied the line of bodies off to the side of the debris line. "The dead will have to be incinerated. There are large predators in this forest. We do not want to attract them."

Ciara gazed up at Taylith. "Cewrick has shielded the area. We cannot move the wounded. They will have to be tended to here. You must bring Laura and the others."

"There is no need to fly back for us." Brenn led his horse to the clearing, the others following him.

Aldis scanned the carnage. "The men are close behind. We will set up camp here."

"How many dead and wounded?" Brenn crossed his arms over his chest, his mouth set in a grim line.

Taylith clenched his jaw. "Roughly two hundred and fifty dead and sixty or more wounded. The injured men cannot be moved. Liana and I will incinerate the dead." He turned to Laura. "Jason, the other medics, and Ciara will need your help with the wounded."

"I will need you, too, Taylith. There are too many for just Jason, Laura, and I."

Taylith nodded. "I will join you after I assist Liana."

Liana grasped Taylith's arm. "I can handle the dead on my own, Taylith. Help them tend to the men."

Taylith brushed his hand over his brow. They had been at it for a couple of hours. The gods had allowed them two of Ciara's flowers. It was more than they could have asked for. Jason had taken them and made a salve to use on the most severe wounds. Luckily, the gods did not limit his own healing capabilities. They were not as extensive as Ciara's, but the flowers would stabilize the severely wounded, giving Jason and the other medics the time they needed to save lives.

They had worked diligently, first tending the men that were near death, then moving on to the others. Many of the injured were engineered soldiers. They would regenerate and heal automatically and be fine by the next morning.

After applying some of the salve Jason had made to a wounded soldier's cuts and scrapes, he glanced at Laura. She was working on one of the last of the men, her face was pale, and her body trembling. He stepped behind her and placed his hands on her shoulders, offering her his strength. She had learned quickly how to use the powers I Am had given her, and to his surprise, she was able to siphon his when her magick began to drain.

Laura released the man she was working on and leaned her back against him. "I think I am all tapped out."

Ciara approached and gestured to the man Laura had healed. "He was the last one. That is all we can do now. The rest of their healing is in the gods and goddesses' hands."

Brenn stepped through the tent flap of their makeshift hospital and pinned them with a hard look. "The three of you, go eat and rest." He turned his gaze to Jason. "You and your helpers, too. The lot of you have been at it for hours. If no lives are in danger, let the medics handle the rest for now. You can return to your duties after you have eaten."

Jason looked as though he was about to argue, but Brenn silenced him. "The king's orders. Join the team by the fire. There is warm food waiting."

CHAPTER TWENTY-ONE

Taylith thought the trek through the Vlolf Mountains would never end. When Brenn finally announced that the last of the mountains were in sight, he heaved a sigh of relief. Thankfully, they had been able to skirt the Dreaded Peaks.

Spring was upon them. The tops of the mountains still had snow on them, but the rest of the land was clear. Trees were sprouting new growth, grass turning green. Spring flowers in abundance dotted throughout the grassy expanse. Birds sang and chirped. Herds of korobeast grazed peacefully as the troops passed them, sometimes startled and fleeing at the invasion of their peaceful existence.

They had not encountered any more of Zohmes' minions. Besides a horse occasionally sliding in the mud, their trek had continued uneventfully, much to their relief. They could do without all the drama.

Taylith gazed up at the sky and spotted the glistening purple-mauve and golden glow of Ciara and Liana's dragons. They had returned from scouting, then landed in the clearing in front of them and shifted. It was uncanny how much their humans resembled each other, but it made sense. They looked like their fathers.

Brenn held up his hand, halting the troops. "Is all clear up ahead?"

The two women mounted their horses. Ciara nodded. "Up to the mountains, it is. Beyond that last ridge is the Xavena Realm and a large open veld. Zohmes and Odoxon are camped there. They have thousands of warriors getting ready for battle."

Brenn cast her a sidelong glance. "I hope they did not see you."

"No, we flew very high. They would just think we were two birds," Liana said and grinned.

"Pretty birds," Taylith commented.

"They are beautiful." Laura's horse whinnied and dug its hooves in the dirt. "If they weren't your sister and cousin, I'd be jealous."

"The mountain pass is clear, but Zohmes and Odoxon can see us coming if we use it and the road," Ciara warned.

"Then we will need to avoid the pass and descend the mountain under the cover of trees. We cannot risk them surprising us," Brenn decided.

"We'd be sitting ducks if we use the road," Erica added.

Brenn turned to look at Erica. "Sitting ducks?"

"Another Earth saying."

"When we camp this evening, we must discuss strategy," Biryn said.

"Yes, definitely. We should reach the summit by nightfall. Those are merely hills and will be easy to scale. We will camp just before the summit, and no campfires. We don't want to alert Zohmes with our smoke if we can help it."

Taylith snorted. "I doubt if we will have the element of surprise. Zohmes and Odoxon seem to know our every move."

As Brenn had predicted, they reached the summit just before nightfall. Daylight was getting longer now that spring had shown its nose. They set up camp just below the summit and decided not to set up the tents. Their skin suits would keep them warm enough during the milder night.

Brenn placed a glimmer stick on the ground. They sat in a circle around it, munching on some roasted but cold meat. Taylith looked at Brenn. "I think we should scout again. I will go with the women this time."

"Let us discuss strategy first. I thought about a plan of attack while we rode. We are going to sleep early and get up after midnight, descend the mountain under tree cover, then attack while it is still dark. They will not expect us during the night."

Biryn nodded. "I think that is a good strategy. They will be completely caught off guard. Zohmes probably knows we are very close and will expect the attack tomorrow, during daylight."

"Stealth is of the utmost importance. Once we step foot on the open veld, their guards will spot us. But when they sound the alarm, Zohmes' troops will be completely unprepared and Zohmes and Odoxon will not have time to organize formation of their troops. Fifty of our troops will remain under the cover of the forest as our reserve." Brenn handed his wineskin to Erica.

"This will be full-scale battle. I do not think the women should be involved and they should remain here," Biryn suggested.

Ciara laughed. "Liana and I are dragons and we have our magick. First, you are going to need us. Second, we can hold our own."

Brenn scrunched his forehead. "Do not think you can just rain dragon fire on their army. Odoxon and Zohmes will have it well protected. Do not forget we are dealing with the most powerful sorcerer ever and a god. Erica and Astiana, you two are to stay here, too."

"Like hell I will. You seem to forget, you need the four swords, and mine happens to be one of them." Erica stated firmly.

Biryn heaved a big sigh. "There is no arguing with these women, but Ciara is correct, we need their magick, and we need the four swords."

"I have eaten and am going to scout. Are you coming, Liana? Taylith?" Ciara asked.

"Be careful," Brenn warned.

Taylith sent him a frown. "I found a small clearing earlier. There is enough room for us to shift, one at a time."

The three dragons returned quite fast. Liana and Ciara sat on the ground while Taylith remained standing. "Many of them are feasting. Their campfires burn brightly. It is almost as if they are celebrating a victory that has not yet happened."

"Good. That means a lot of them are most probably drunk with wine and spirits. Their reactions will be slow, and they will be disoriented." Brenn chuckled.

Taylith grunted. "It will take a lot of wine and spirits to get some of those giants drunk."

"Nevertheless, too much alcohol dulls the senses, even if they are not completely drunk," Erica said.

"Laro, Ivran, Aldis, send word to the captains to pass our plan of strategy down the lines. Our horses stay here. Fifty troops will remain under cover of the forest while the rest of us attack. Aldis will sound the horn three times when the reserves can swoop in. Tell our archers to aim their fire arrows for the tents," Brenn ordered and held up his hand. "A spring shower. We need to set up the tents after all. And now, time to rest for a few hours."

The men quickly set up their tent. Taylith snuggled close to Laura. He kissed her briefly, then whispered, "I love you so much. Stay by my side tomorrow. Promise."

"I will. Let us pray for victory. I can't wait to go home and lead a normal life."

Taylith laughed softly. "And how boring will that be? Will our life ever be dull? As long as Zohmes and Odoxon plague us, we will never have a tranquil moment. Now try to sleep, my love."

Fortunately, it was only a shower. When they got up the next morning and prepared for battle, the rain had stopped.

They hid behind trees. The veld stretched beyond Zohmes' camp not that far from the edge of the forest. Brenn led the first charge. Fires still burned brightly among the many tents, but all seemed quiet.

The archers sent their arrows to the tents. They ignited instantly. Zohmes' warriors came running out of them, some of them on fire. The loud sound of drums echoed throughout the valley. As Brenn had predicted, it was chaos in Zohmes' camp. All manner of warriors, if one could call them that, his creatures, and the Yeavoth, ran in disorder through the campsite.

Brenn, flanked by the other men, ran ahead. The first of Zohmes' warriors had come to their senses somewhat and began to attack the invaders.

Taylith recognized their black armor from his vision, the spiked helmets. They carried long, sharp spikes. Green tendrils of magick snaked around their bodies. He wished he could call out his dragon, but that would be going against Brenn's orders. He tried to keep Laura by his side, but there were so many misshapen warriors attacking them now, he lost track of her. No time to panic. Fleet weapon in one hand, his sword in the other, he killed one creature after another. The green snake spell was no match against his magick sword.

The drums sounded again. More and more of Zohmes' minions attacked. Suddenly a blinding green light caused him to lose his footing. He fell. A spear descended toward his chest, but someone thwarted the attack on him. He scrambled up just in time to catch Ivran, who was fatally wounded in the chest, the monster's spear still protruding from it.

Ivran had saved his life, but only by forfeiting his own. Taylith's heart thumped as he sat on the ground, cradling Ivran against him. Tears ran down his cheeks unheeded. "Ivran, my friend. Do not leave us. Ivran, stay with me," he shouted.

The spear had gone straight through. If he tried to remove it, Ivran would bleed out. He moved his bloodied hand to Ivran's neck and checked for a pulse. There was none. He grabbed a handful of the small blue flowers now blooming on the ground next to him where his tears had fallen, then packed them around the wound. Deep down he knew his flowers would not be enough to save Ivran's life.

Laura…his vision…

Wildly, he looked among the throng of fighters and finally spotted her. *Laura, I need you. Laura, can you hear me?* Gods, he hoped they were not too late.

She nailed the warrior she'd been fighting, then turned and saw him. *I am coming.* He watched her run toward them. Then she kneeled beside him.

"Lay him down, Taylith."

"I think he has gone." His voice broke and he let out a sob. "He is not breathing."

While stroking Ivran's hair, watching the lifeblood drain

from his chest, he saw Laura place her hands on the spear. They began to glow brightly as she bent the spear and broke it. More blood gushed from Ivran's chest. "Laura, it is no use. His lifeblood is draining from his body. Ivran has left us."

"No...I can feel his spirit. I can save him." She turned Ivran onto his chest. The spearhead protruded from his back. Gently, she began to remove the spear from Ivran's body.

One of Zohmes' warriors leaped toward him. Taylith jumped up, fury now overwhelming his grief. He struck the creature with his sword, the blade slicing the head off cleanly. It fell to the ground, green fluid oozing from its severed neck. He turned back to stand guard over Laura and Ivran when he saw her place both hands over the wound. Her hands now glowing like the brightest star he had ever seen, her body shimmered in the dark of the night, and she closed her eyes. For moments she sat like that, then turned Ivran over and did the same to the chest wound.

Ivran suddenly sat up, rubbed his chest, looking at Laura and up at Taylith. "That creature had a mighty punch. Come, we cannot sit here and be idle."

Taylith trembled at what he had just witnessed. Ivran acted like nothing had happened and joined the fighters. He pulled himself together and just in time as a Yeavoth came for him. It was the giant black man from his vision, a silver braid dangling from his head.

"Here come the Wookies," he heard Erica shout.

There was no time to wonder what she meant, but he presumed she was referring to the ape-like creatures that appeared out of nowhere.

He fought like a maniac against the giant black man. Because he was so much smaller, he was also faster and could avoid the man's thrusts. It was Dronko, the ruler of the Yeavoth. "Dronko, why are you doing this?" he yelled at the man. "I thought you were in alliance with the king."

"Biryn broke his promises. The guaranteed equipment never arrived."

"You stupid fool! Your ships are under construction, but we have been busy against Zohmes and Odoxon. They are nothing but evil. What in the gods' names is wrong with you?" Taylith lunged at Dronko, his sword finding purchase in the large man's thigh. A burst of power flowed through him, down his arms and hands. The blade of his sword glowed brightly.

Dronko staggered and suddenly stopped fighting, then pointed his sword at the ground. He gazed down at Taylith, a look of confusion in his eyes. "You are sure of this?"

Taylith held his sword ready. "Yes. I swear on the lives of all my loved ones."

Dronko dropped his sword to the ground, shaking his head as if he were trying to clear it. "I think I made a mistake."

Taylith took a step back when Dronko reached for his belt and withdrew a horn. He sounded it. It had a different sound than Brenn's horn, much louder, almost deafening. The hairy ape-like creatures stopped their fight against the Ierilians and looked at Dronko.

"We are fighting for the king!" Dronko shouted loudly. His men and warriors now turned on Zohmes' minions.

Panic attacked Taylith when he noticed Laura was not near him. His gaze traveled over the fighting throng. He spotted her finally, desperately fighting close to Biryn. He stumbled over dead bodies and bleeding limbs in his haste to get to them.

The blinding green light shone again, this time illuminating the whole camp. A tall figure stood in its midst. It was Odoxon enlarged to a giant. He lifted his gnarled black staff and pointed the black dragon top at Biryn. "Biryn, watch out!" Taylith yelled.

He need not have feared. Cewrick faced Odoxon. By his side, Liana and Icaras. Between the three of them, their hands held out, their fingers spewing fire, they chanted and thwarted whatever spell Odoxon was using.

The man shrank again to his normal size. Zohmes' face appeared above the fighting mass, his hair resembling flames as it blew wildly, his eyes a glowing red. Red bolts issued from his eyes, slaying not only the Ierilians, but also some of his own warriors.

Aldis' horn sounded three times. Taylith knew he was calling on the reserves.

Daylight broke. The air was putrid with the stench of smoke and blood. Many of the warriors were still fighting. Taylith was relieved to see that the slain on the ground were mainly Zohmes' minions. Yes, there were slain Ierilians, but not as many as he had feared. He was exhausted but would fight to the bitter end. Zohmes' warriors were thinning fast. The god and the sorcerer watched them from a distance now, not partaking in the battle. *Surely they must see their army is losing?*

He dealt a kill blow to a half-man, half-reptilian creature, when Zohmes and Odoxon stepped among the last of the fighters. Liana surged toward them, Jonathan running beside her.

Taylith yelled, "Liana! Jonathan! No!" They did not listen to him.

Liana held her hands out, her forefinger pointing at Odoxon. She chanted loudly. Her body took on the appearance of a vortex of fire as she hurled herself at Odoxon.

Jonathan stood next to Liana. Power swirled around him in a whirlwind of black smoke and flame. His body glowed like a supernova. He raised his hands, shooting flames from his fingertips directed at Zohmes.

Liana had taken Odoxon by surprise. His screams echoed through the valley. Could she really kill the old man? When the vortex of flame stopped, the sorcerer had disappeared.

Zohmes screamed in fury. His army had been thwarted and Odoxon had been defeated. He pinned Jonathan with an angry glare as he warded off the fire Jonathan directed at him. A menacing grin suddenly split his face. Maniacal laughter echoed through the veld as the god vanished in a flash of fire and smoke.

A sick feeling pooled in Taylith's belly. Could Zohmes have guessed that Jonathan was his son? He heard Aldis' horn sound one long bellow to signal the end of the battle. He gazed over the battlefield. The veld was covered with bodies, the ground stained with blood and all colors of slime oozing from Zohmes' slain creatures. Brenn's men combed the valley, assisting the wounded Ierilians or finishing off the creatures that had formed Zohmes' army.

He joined the team as they made their way to Liana and Jonathan.

Laura sidled up to him and slid her hand in his. Her face was pale, and she was covered in blood and grime. All of them were. He turned his attention to Brenn. "As soon as your men clear the field of any of our wounded, Ciara, Liana, and I will incinerate the dead."

"Ivran, you look like a train wreck. What in the hell did you do to your armor?" Erica cocked her head at Ivran.

Taylith glanced at Ivran. He did look pretty bad. His clothing and chainmail were caked with blood and his armor had a large hole in the center of the chest where the spear had pierced him, as well as one in the back where it had exited.

"I have no idea. A spear must have caught it." He

examined his clothing.

"And the blood? Are you sure you're not hurt?" Erica persisted.

Ivran felt his chest. "No. Must be someone else's blood."

Taylith glanced at Laura, who winked and shook her head slightly. They could tell him later. He turned and watched the remainder of Zohmes' minions flee to the distant forest and mountains. They had won the war. But at what cost? His heart felt heavy for those that had given their lives to save their world and the crown.

CHAPTER TWENTY-TWO

The sound of the warriors' merrymaking filled the silence of the veld. Though the battle had been harsh, and everyone was weary, the team joined in the celebration.

"To victory!" Brenn shouted, holding up his wineskin.

Taylith held up his wineskin. "To those that gave their life. May they dwell peacefully in the realm of dreams."

"Aye, aye," Laura said, then drank from her wineskin.

Ivran grimaced and pulled at his armor. "The first stream we come to tomorrow, I'm going to wash all this grime off my body and clothing. I do not care if it is melted snow run-off and ice cold."

Jonathan scowled. "So Odoxon has been defeated, but Zohmes still lives."

Liana munched on some meat. "Odoxon is back on Wuits Peak in his cave. We cannot kill him."

Erica laughed sarcastically and shook her head. "And you really think he'll stay there? You watch, Zohmes will rescue him again and restore his powers."

Brenn passed his wineskin to Biryn, then pulled Ciara onto his lap. "Zohmes suffered big losses today. The army he engineered has dwindled to almost nothing. Let us hope he needs a lot of time to recover from this defeat. We leave at first light. Our journey home should be much faster now that the snow is melting. I estimate we will be home in a few weeks."

Biryn took a drink from the wineskin and gazed at the fire. "Let us pray to the gods that Zohmes' recovery of his losses takes a very long time."

Jonathan seated himself beside Liana. She grinned and handed him a stick with meat. Was it Taylith's imagination or did he see more than just friendliness in Jonathan's eyes? Now that would be interesting. The woman Odoxon coveted in his younger days, and Zohmes' spawn? They would make a formidable couple with their combined magick and powers. He shook his head and groped for Laura's hand. "Sweetness, every bone in my body is aching. How about—"

She twined her fingers with his. "Yes, I hear you. Let's go to the tent. I am beat."

They laid their bedrolls next to each other, but in reality only needed one. Taylith took his mate into his arms and held her tight. He felt so proud of her. She had fought and stood her ground like the best of warriors, and when Ivran was wounded, the magick she had been gifted with had restored his heartbeat and healed his deadly wound. Her lips grazed his cheek. When he gazed down at her, her eyes were closed, and she breathed steady.

At first light, the sound of the troops getting ready to depart woke him. Surprised, he found Laura already gone, her bedroll neatly rolled, ready to put on the packhorse.

Running his fingers through his grimy hair, he stumbled out of the tent. The camp was a flurry of activity. Some were still eating, others were dismantling the tents and packing up.

He quickly relieved himself, then joined the team around the fire. Ivran handed him a stick with meat.

"I already hunted and caught two korobeasts. Everyone had fresh roasted meat this morning." He grinned. "Now that we are rested, can anyone tell me if they saw what happened for me to get my armor so damaged? How my clothes are soaked with blood?"

"Ivran, you might recall I did not want Laura to go with us. The night before we departed, I had a vision. In the vision I was told that Laura had to go, and it showed me you severely wounded and dying. Then I saw Laura removing the spear from your body and healing you. The gift bestowed on her is miraculous. She brought you back from the dead. You had no heartbeat and I thought we had lost you," Taylith told him softly.

Ivran took off his armor, pulled up his chainmail and tunic, and showed them his unblemished chest. "There is no mark on my skin."

Taylith laced his fingers with Laura's. "Believe me, if I had not witnessed this miracle with my own eyes, I would not believe it."

Astiana smiled at Laura. "I Am named Laura the keeper of souls when he bestowed her the power of healing. She truly can hold the dying to life."

Erica chimed in. "That means Laura can heal anyone?"

Ciara shook her head. "No. Only as it is written in the book of knowledge. It was not Ivran's time to travel to the realm of dreams."

Liana threw her empty stick on the fire. "Brenn, Aldis, when you send in your reports, can you not say anything about me? I would like to confront my parents in person, with Taylith."

Brenn frowned. "It will be a big shock. A warning would be better, I think."

"Please? We do not know if we will encounter anything on the journey home. Once we are safely in Cront, Taylith and I will fly home. That is if Laura does not mind?"

Taylith looked at Laura, then at Liana. "Can she not come? She is your sister now. And Ciara and Brenn should be present, too. We are family."

Liana looked thoughtful. "Yes, I agree. I am sorry. I have been alone for so many centuries, to be around people is a strange sensation, but a very welcome one. Of course, Brenn, Ciara, and Laura must come. You are now all my family."

"Aldis and I will not mention you in our reports when we send word this morning that we were victorious. You have my word," Brenn promised.

"On a more serious note. Do we have a count of our losses?" Aldis asked.

"Yes. The captains of each troop have reported their losses. We lost nine hundred and eighty-two men. Five hundred and thirteen were engineered warriors," Brenn answered. "But Zohmes lost a lot more. I would be surprised if he had a hundred warriors left."

"The wounded?"

"Have all been tended to. Between Jason, his medics, Ciara, Taylith, and Laura, they are all able to travel."

Biryn stood. "I, for one, cannot wait to go home to my queen. Are we ready to move on?"

"And I can't wait to have you all to myself." Laura pecked Taylith on the cheek.

"Enough of that," Icaras growled. "Help me with the tent, Taylith?"

They had ridden for a few hours when they came upon a

stream. Chunks of ice floated on its waters, but it looked crystal clear. "I think it's time for a bath," Laura shouted and pulled on the reins to stop her horse.

Brenn held up his hand. "You might be right, though this water is going to be very cold."

"You think I give a flying fuck?" Laura said and promptly dismounted and headed for the stream, followed by the other women.

They removed their armor and chainmail but kept the rest of their clothing on. To take off their clothes with thousands of soldiers around them was not a good plan.

Taylith followed Laura into the water. The icy cold took his breath away, but once his body got used to it, it actually felt warmer than he had expected. He dunked his head, rinsed his hair, and watched Laura do the same.

"Goddamn, I feel so much cleaner now," Laura muttered as she waded out to the bank.

They had no towels to dry off, so they sought out whatever sunny spots they could find to semi-dry and with the help of their fleet weapons.

"I almost hate putting on this chainmail and armor again," Laura complained. "It's filthy dirty. Do I really still need to wear it?"

"Yes, love. We have no idea if we will encounter anything on the way home."

"Good God, I hope not. That war was enough to last me a lifetime." Laura swung her hair back and forth in an attempt to shake out the excess water.

"I hope you feel cleaner now," Taylith said.

"I do. Sort of half clean. I've never longed so much for a bath in my life." Laura headed back to her horse, but Brenn had issued the order for a break.

Taylith helped to gather firewood and they built a fire, all of them sitting close to it to dry their clothes.

They were sitting a little way from the others. Laura nudged him. "Honey, what do you think of Liana's plan to shock the living daylights out of your parents?"

"I do not agree with it. Father and Mother will be stunned. But on the other hand, I resent I was never told of the sister I had. We have to leave it up to Liana. It is her choice and decision."

"Your parents must be really old. Can they withstand such a trauma? Won't they die on the spot?"

Taylith laughed. "Laura, dragons are very strong. No shock can cause death. Like I said, this is how Liana wants to proceed and we have to honor her wishes."

They moved closer to the fire. Brenn announced a greeting from the queen. "Biryn, Cylena is eagerly looking forward to your return. Cront is celebrating our victory. She says the little prince is kicking up a storm."

Biryn laughed. "Yes, I just got the same message."

The journey down the pass was much easier than it had been during the month of frost. The snow was completely melted, the trees were covered in newly formed leaves, the ground carpeted in lush green grasses, and the forest dotted with a myriad of brightly colored flowers.

Taylith studied the tree line in front of them. Beyond them would be the base of the mountain where they had rested after their first battle. Brenn was right—what had taken them months this winter to travel had only taken weeks. They were almost to Cront.

Luckily, there had been no attacks. Zohmes had been silent since he had tucked tail and vanished from the battlefield, though it still bothered Taylith the way the god had looked at Jonathan.

"We will rest beyond the trees," Brenn called out. "We will reach Cront tonight."

Cheers rose up around them, echoing through the forest as the men received the news.

Laura pulled back slightly on her horse's reins and grinned up at Taylith. "We are almost home! I can't believe it. Hot bath here I come!"

Gods she was beautiful, even if they were filthy from the long weeks of travel. *A hot bath and finally a night alone with my beautiful mate.* He smiled and winked at her.

Heat flared in those sparkling green eyes. *Keep it up, studmuffin. I have been aching to get you alone for months.*

CHAPTER TWENTY-THREE

Taylith held Laura in his arms. She was still in a deep sleep. By the time they had reached the palace it was late in the evening. The moons had hung heavy in the sky, and everyone was sound asleep except for the guards posted at the entrance.

After he and Laura reached their room and finished bathing the grime from their bodies, exhaustion had set in. They both had fallen into a deep slumber by the time their heads hit the pillows, the bed a luxury they had been denied for months.

Taylith gazed down at Laura's beautiful face. The suns' rays spilled through the window, making her hair look like spun gold. He took a strand of it between his fingers, toying with its silky softness. Gods, he wanted nothing more than to explore every inch of her alabaster skin. It had been months since they had been alone, and every inch of him was on fire with need. He took a deep breath to tamp it down. His mate needed the rest and they had plenty of time to make up for lost time.

He kissed her tenderly on the cheek. The war had changed them both. The gods did not pair souls that were not equally matched. His mate had grown into a fierce warrior who could hold her own on the battlefield – a healer with miraculous power. And he had learned to allow her the freedom to become the woman she was destined to be.

She shifted and opened her eyes, her body stretching languorously against him. "Mmmm...I have missed waking up next to you like this. Why didn't you wake me sooner?"

"You needed the sleep." He leaned down, seeking her lips, and whispered, "It is not that late yet."

Her passion-filled gaze locked with his. "God, Taylith, it has been so long. I need you...now."

She skimmed her fingers from his chest, down his abdomen, then straddled his hips. She grasped his aching cock and guided it to her slick opening. With one thrust of her hips, she had seated herself to the hilt.

Hunger drove them both, their bodies ravenous. He grasped her hips, meeting her movements thrust for thrust until her cries of pleasure filled the air. Her body spasmed around him. He pulled her down, kissing her hard, and let her carry him into oblivion and sweet release.

Laura collapsed against him, kissing his neck and chest, then peered up at him. "I love you."

He kissed the top of her head. "I love you, too, sweetness." He held her for a few moments longer, enjoying the feel of her skin against his. He shifted them to their sides and checked his timepiece. "We should bathe and dress. We have about fifteen minutes before we are to meet the others in Biryn's chambers."

Laura groaned and snuggled closer to him. "After this, promise me... One day all to ourselves. At home. Maybe the bed will be fixed."

He chuckled and pulled her from the bed. "After the cold ground for so many months, the mattress on the floor will suit me fine."

They bathed and dressed quickly, then made their way to Biryn's quarters. Luckily, they were not the last ones to arrive. Jonathan and Liana met them at the king's door.

Liana scrunched her nose at Taylith. "Jonathan was kind enough to show me the way. I was quite lost. This place is huge."

They entered the king's chambers. Cewrick, Hirsuta, Brenn, and Ciara were already seated at the table waiting for them. Biryn was just guiding Cylena to her seat.

After seating himself beside the queen, Biryn rested his hand on her protruding belly and ginned. "Our little prince is very active."

Cylena nodded. "Yes, he does not stay still." She cast a curious glance around the table. "Where is the rest of the team?"

Brenn took a sip from his cup. "Ivran, Aldis, Erica, and Laro returned home when we arrived in Cront to be with their families. They will return to the palace soon."

"Now that I have seen Liana safely to the king's chambers, I'm off to surprise my mother." Jonathan gave Liana a lopsided grin as he left the room.

They seated themselves at the table with the others. The kitchen staff had already brought food and laid it out, and a carafe stood on each end of the table.

Laura took a deep breath, sniffed, and smiled, then pointed to one of the carafes. "Oh my God! Is that coffee?"

Dunmore quickly poured a cup and brought it to Laura. "It is from the first harvest of your coffee bean plants. The plants seem to thrive very well in our soil."

"The soil enhancement has sure helped. On Earth we would have had to wait a few more years. Thank the gods for your enhanced technology," Laura said while sniffing in the aroma from her cup.

"We can be even more thankful to the gods and goddesses for helping us attain our victory and bringing the team home safely." Biryn sent them all a grateful smile. "Thank you all. Words cannot portray how deeply thankful I am for my family. I hope we can all enjoy a reprieve from Zohmes and Odoxon's games."

"First on my to-do list this morning—accompany Liana to Storming Enclave, with Ciara, Brenn, and Laura." Taylith helped himself to eggs.

Biryn frowned. "Liana, I really wish you would let me inform your parents. It is going to be a big shock for them."

Liana raised a delicate brow. "As big a shock as it was for Taylith to discover *them* still alive? Yes, he told me the whole tale of Blood Lagoon and the black dragons. No. I appreciate your offer, but I would like to do this on my own."

"Our parents will find out soon enough. We leave for Storming Enclave after breakfast." Taylith was anxious to escort his sister back home and find out why his parents had never told him about her.

Jonathan returned with Julia and ushered her to the table. She looked a little shocked when she noticed Liana.

After a quick explanation they finished their breakfast and said their goodbyes.

When they reached the courtyard, Taylith, Liana, and Ciara shifted into their dragons.

Taylith kneeled for Laura to climb on his back while Brenn climbed onto Ciara's. *Are you girls ready for this?*

Liana nudged him with her snout. *As ready as I will ever be to face Father and Mother after I disregarded their warnings. I was so rebellious when I was young.*

Taylith heard Ciara's tinkling laughter in his mind. *It runs in the family.* He spread his wings and leaped into the air. Liana and Ciara followed behind.

Liana slowed when she flew beside him, Ciara continuing to climb. Then she turned and dove back toward them. He chuckled. His cousin wished to play.

Taylith shielded Laura with magick to keep her seated. *Hold tight, sweetness.* He surged upward, meeting Ciara nose to nose, almost touching, then dove below her and rolled, Laura's squeals of laughter echoing in his ears. His mate was a little daredevil and loved flying just as much as he did.

They played a while longer, Liana joining the fun before settling in beside each other, a straight flight to Storming Enclave.

Halfway to their destination, Taylith contacted his father. He would at least give them a warning that he and Laura were on their way to visit them. They had not spoken since before they left for war. *Father, Laura and I are on the way to Storming Enclave to spend a few hours with you. We should be there soon.* Jelano's surprised voice sounded in his mind.

We heard of your victory but did not know you had made it back to Cront. We are proud of you, son, and will celebrate your victory and return.

When Storming Enclave came in sight, Liana picked up speed. Taylith and Ciara kept pace with her. Taylith knew after all this time she was eager to see their parents. They landed in the courtyard close to the castle. Taylith and Ciara kneeled to allow their mates to slide off their backs. Then the dragons changed to their humans.

Liana grabbed Taylith's hand. "I am so nervous."

Taylith pulled her into his arms and hugged her. "There is nothing to be nervous about. Mother and Father will be happy to know you are alive and well."

Ciara slid her arms around them both. When they released each other, she held one of Liana's hands. "We do this together. You are not alone anymore."

They hurried to the castle entrance. Someone must have notified Taylith's parents of their arrival. They were standing in the doorway, waiting for them.

Jelano caught his mate just as her knees buckled. Copera's face turned very pale. Her hand flew to her mouth, and her blue eyes glistened with tears. His father looked as though he had seen a ghost. He may as well have. Liana had been gone for so many centuries.

The shock on his mother's face gave way to pure joy. She took a faltering step, then ran to meet them, her face soaked from the tears that continued like a waterfall. She stopped just in front of Liana, then reached out to touch her cheek, a look of disbelief on her face. "Liana, is it really you?"

Liana threw her arms around Copera, tears streaming down her face. "Yes, it really is."

Jelano hugged them both. Taylith stood back, not wanting to interrupt Liana's reunion with their parents. When his father stepped back he looked at Taylith. "How is this possible?"

Brenn and Laura had stood quietly in the background. "We should go inside, and we can tell you everything," Brenn suggested.

"Good plan, Brenn. Wait, I want to contact Brokig and Iede. I would like them to be here." Jelano stepped aside for a moment to contact his brother. He turned back to them. "They will be here shortly. Now, let us go in. We have refreshments waiting. Daughter, come here. I would like to hold you in my arms again and feel that you are real."

"Father, there is so much to talk about. Taylith has already told me a lot about what has been happening on Ierilia, but I—"

"My princess, wait until your aunt and uncle are here. Now come along."

Jelano led them to their personal living quarters. Along the way, servants stopped in hallways to gape at Liana. They had barely sat when King Brokig and Iede came in. Like his brother, Brokig's face turned a deathly white and Iede grasped his arm when they saw Liana.

"Liana? But…she is…"

"Presumed dead. Emphasis on the word *presumed*. We never found a trace of her, remember?" Jelano said.

"By the gods. This is…the miracle…of all miracles," Iede stuttered, then approached Liana and embraced her in a death hug.

"It is really me. I am back," Liana said softly, obviously overwhelmed by all the emotion in the room.

Jelano waved his servants out of the room and, picking up a flask, poured wine into their glasses. "A toast to the return of our princess!"

Taylith held his glass up. "Welcome home, Liana. Now that everyone is here, you can begin to tell them where you were and what all happened."

Liana talked for a long time, occasionally interrupted by Taylith, Ciara, Brenn, and Laura, who added their bit.

When she finally finished talking, Brokig said, "I wish we could glimpse into the book of knowledge to see what the future holds."

Taylith shuddered. He had no wish to see more of what the future may hold. The small glimpses he had been given were enough for him, but he knew I Am would continue showing him details of what had been written and what could possibly come.

Ciara glanced at Taylith, understanding in her eyes, then answered her father. "But there are various outcomes of the future. And we all know, everything has to happen as it has been written. Whatever outcome the gods choose, we must abide by it. If we all knew the future, it could harm our destiny considerably. As it stands, what Odoxon did to Liana and our family is unforgivable, but it could have been a lot worse. At least she has survived all these centuries and she is safe now and back with us."

"And she managed to banish Odoxon back to Wuits Peak. I am proud of you, daughter!" Jelano raised his glass to her.

"Liana, now that you are home again, you must learn to restrain your headstrong ways," Copera told her daughter.

Liana chuckled. "Mother, I am adventurous by nature. I am going to ask King Biryn to add me to his team. I cannot sit idle and embroider tapestries and cushions like most of the ladies at court."

Jelano stood and slammed his glass on the table. "I forbid it!"

Liana laughed again and Taylith had to admire her courage to stand up for herself. "Father, I am centuries old now. I can go and do as I please. I will spend as much time as possible with you and Mother, but I need to lead the life I love, which is a life filled with danger and adventure."

"You are not going to live with us?" Copera asked.

"No, Mother. I will live on Ierilia, but I promise I will visit often."

Brokig pinned Liana with a hard stare, then angrily gestured to Taylith and Ciara. "You will not join your brother and cousin in their foolhardiness. I will not allow it." He shook his head. "The lot of you forget that you are heirs to your own kingdoms."

Taylith took a deep breath. Both Jelano and Brokig were known for their short tempers. Especially if they thought their children had put themselves in harm's way. Brokig's anger could be felt across the Tideless Abyss when Taylith had informed him he would be staying at Brenn's estate. The only thing that had pacified the dragon king was that Taylith would be with Ciara.

"Uncle…you were once a general when Ierilia needed your protection. They need us again." He looked at Liana. "If this is what Liana wishes, she can live with us. Laura and I will watch over her. I promise." He glanced at Laura, hoping she would not mind. He had said it on the spur of the moment. But she merely smiled at him.

Brenn added, "She is also welcome to live with Ciara and me on my estate."

Jelano, now pacing, frowned and looked at his daughter. "We thought you dead. We have mourned you all these years, and now you want to deprive us of your company? It is bad enough that your brother has chosen to live on Ierilia."

"Father, I promise I will visit all the time. But Ierilia is far from being safe from danger. I banished Odoxon to Wuits Peak, but Zohmes carries on. We were victorious in this war, but it is not the end. Zohmes' thirst for rulership of Ierilia continues and his insane battle to put the crown on his head. My powers have increased over the centuries. Yes, they were dormant while I was a miniature dragon, but once I was released from the spell, they returned in full force. I am so much stronger than I ever was when I was very young, and my magick is as strong as Odoxon's, if not more. No one else has been able to banish Odoxon back to his miserable cave on Wuits Peak. Not even Cewrick, who also has mighty powers. King Biryn and his team need me."

"The goddess Rania has confirmed this, Uncle," Ciara told him.

Copera gasped, shock clouding her features. "Ciara, are you telling us that Liana is more powerful than you?"

"Yes. She is so much older, and over the centuries, though she could not use her powers, her magick has developed."

Jelano looked grim as he sat. "We cannot argue with the goddess. So be it. Daughter, I expect you to visit us at least once a week, unless you are away on assignments."

Liana clasped her hands in her lap, her eyes downcast. "Yes, Father."

Taylith looked at Liana's demure expression and laughed inwardly. She was far from the sedate creature that sat before them now. He focused on his parents. "Why was I never told of Liana? You kept this information from me, why?"

"It was very painful for all of us, son. We moved the skies and everything else to find Liana. There was no trace of her, so we all presumed her to have gone to the realm of dreams. The pain of losing Liana ripped us to shreds. We asked that it should never be spoken of again. Centuries later, we were blessed with another child, a son. You."

Taylith clenched his jaw. He understood their pain. He had felt the same when he thought he had lost his parents to the curse. "Can you even imagine what it was like facing a sister I never knew I had?"

"Yes, son. We never told you, or Ciara, because we did not want you to do something rash and begin a search for a sister that had been missing for centuries. You and Ciara are, or used to be, just as reckless as your sister."

Taylith thought about this for a few minutes. "Yes, I suppose you are right. If I had known about Liana, I would have turned Ierilia upside down to find her."

"And involved Ciara in the process," Brokig added.

Ciara scrunched up her face. "Yes, I am sure I would have helped Taylith."

Pain pierced Taylith's skull. He grabbed his head and closed his eyes, bracing himself for the vision that lanced through his mind.

Cylena, lying on the floor, her head cradled in Biryn's lap. Pain

217

contorted the king's features and his hand rested on the large swell of her belly. A sickly green mist surrounded Cylena's body. She appeared to be unconscious. Catrice knelt beside them, her mouth set in a grim line as she searched for a heartbeat, then placed a stethoscope on Cylena's belly. Catrice shook her head, tears soaking her cheeks. A huge black hole in the ground. An old temple. An alien spaceship appearing in the sky, raining fire upon Ierilia. The two look-alike men in battle. Brothers at war. A massive ball of fire followed by a flaming trail hurling toward a distant, small, shadowed planet.

"Taylith! Taylith!"

Someone was shouting his name. It echoed through his mind…distorted as if from a long distance. He rubbed his eyes to clear his vision. The stabbing pain receded, and his sight began to clear, but the image he had seen chilled his blood. Zohmes and Odoxon's harassment was far from over. Much of his vision had come to pass, but a lot was still in store for them. The most important part of the vision—the queen and her infant were in danger. "We must return to the palace now!"

NEXT IN THIS SERIES:

INITIATION GENESIS

Starting anew on an alien planet, is no mean task — especially if that planet is rife with magic, shapeshifters, dragons, not to mention a fallen evil god, and a villainous sorcerer.

Now that the king and queen have granted the people from Earth their own realm, Bernie Henderson has been elected to rule it and oversee the building of their new city.

Zohmes and Odoxon have not given up. Bernie finds himself immersed in the trials and tribulations of Ierilia. How will this affect his budding interest in Julia, the mother of Zohmes' son?

EXCERPT INITIATION GENESIS:

Julia, Cylena, and Hirsuta were still in their robes when lunch was served.

"My heart is heavy for the families of the men who lost their lives," Cylena said as she helped herself to some bread and cheese. "It feels wrong for us to be so happy to be reunited while others are grieving."

"Has Catrice given any indication when we can expect our little prince?" Biryn asked Cylena, changing the subject.

She smiled. "Any time. Now that we have heard all the stories of your journey and the war, I think I would like to bathe and get dressed."

"You have hardly eaten, Cylena." Biryn stood and held her arm as she got up off her chair.

Julia noticed Cylena grimace, pull a face, and clutch her back. "She's going into labor!"

Before Biryn had a chance to lead her to the bedroom, Cylena crumpled to the floor. "Call Catrice!" he shouted.

A sickly green mist appeared, enveloping Cylena. Biryn cradled her head in his lap. Astiana, Icaras, Cewrick, and Hirsuta rushed to the queen, Cewrick chanting a spell, but it did not remove the green fog.

Julia's heart thudded against her ribs. "My God. Jonathan, can you do something?"

Catrice came rushing in, followed by Jason carrying a stretcher. "What the hell is all this green stuff? Incense? Get rid of it! Place her on the stretcher. We need to take her to the infirmary."

They ran through the hallways, the green mist swirling around the gurney. Once in the clinic, Catrice and Jason shifted Cylena to a bed. Julia watched from the door as Catrice took out her stethoscope and listened to Cylena's heart. Then, placing it on her belly, she listened for the infant's heartbeat. Lifting Cylena's eyelids, she shone a small flashlight at the pupils. Tears soaked her cheeks as she stepped back and shook her head. "Too late. They're both gone." Placing her hand on Biryn's back, she said softly, "Biryn, I am so sorry. There is nothing we can do."

Biryn roared. He gathered Cylena into his arms and sobbed. "Nooooo! This cannot be happening."

Julia had not even noticed Taylith and the others had returned and joined them. Laura pushed her way through and rushed to Cylena's side. Julia watched in awe as her sister placed her hand on the still woman's heart and her other hand on her distended belly. Her hands glowed bright enough to light up the small room. Even Laura's body began to glow, the light cutting right through the green mist.

Cylena suddenly took a deep breath and another. Catrice placed the stethoscope on her chest and nodded. "I have a heartbeat." Then she listened for the baby's and nodded again. "The infant's heart is beating strongly."

"But she is not waking." Biryn's voice was hoarse with emotion.

"Biryn, I don't know, but it almost appears as if Cylena is in hibernation, in stasis," Catrice told him.

Julia grasped Jonathan's hand. "Zohmes."

"Can you wake her from it?" Biryn wrung his hands.

"I've got no idea what this green mist is. Honestly, I don't know if our medicine can fix this." Catrice looked mortified as she talked to the king.

"I need to consult with Rania," Ciara said from somewhere behind them.

"Let's leave them alone," Julia suggested. "Cylena is in good hands."

BOOKS IN THE CRIMSON REALM SERIES:

In Search of Pride – Book 1

The Dragon's Lion – Book 2

Sword of Betrayal – Book 3

Sword of Judgement – Book 4

Testing the Crown – Book 5

Shard in the Mirror – Book 6

Initiation Genesis – Book 7

Tabeka's Revenge – Book 8

Also available, **THE LION'S STOWAWAY**, a novella based on the Ierilian world and its characters, published in an anthology with Viola Grace and other authors. Buy it at extasybooks.com and please help to support the authors by purchasing directly from the publisher!

EXCERPT:

Heading back on the familiar trail, that she could almost walk blindfolded now, she hummed a tune. That was something she missed. Music.

When she was close to her tree, a sound startled her. It was too loud to be made by one of the little furry creatures she so often saw darting around among the flowers. She stopped. Her heart sped up. She'd seen no other human in the forest since she'd lived there. Not once. The sound came from the direction of the crate.

Standing very still, she held her breath and waited. A crack, then another. Suddenly a huge lion faced her. She dropped her basket, her purchases spilling to the forest floor, screamed, and ran to the nearest tree.

She peeked at the lion from behind the trunk and started hitching up her skirts to tie them in a knot above her knees. "Go away, kitty!"

She hoisted herself onto a branch and started climbing. When she was halfway up the tree, she dared to look down. She couldn't remember. Did lions climb?

"Nice kitty, kitty, kitty." She climbed a couple more limbs but dared not go any higher. The branches were starting to get thin and might break beneath her weight. She leaned forward and peered down at the lion.

"Holy shit! You are one big cat!"

He was the biggest lion she'd ever seen. Their parents had taken them to a zoo when she and Hannah were still little. The lions had awed her and had seemed gigantic. But this one was huge. Of course, he had to be. It was an alien lion.

What in the hell was she going to do? Was it hungry? Was it looking at her for its next meal? She grabbed the piece of smoked meat she had in her pocket, pulled a chunk off it with her teeth and held her hand out. "Look, kitty. Mmm, it's good, see?"

She threw the piece of meat. It landed on the ground a distance from the tree. "Go get it, boy!"

The lion just stood looking up at her. He did not attempt to climb or approach the tree...nor did he go after the food. To her consternation, he suddenly growled. Then it appeared as if his bones were popping through his skin.

"Oh, fuck, no!"

It freaked her the hell out. It was like the movie *Thing*. An alien made itself look like a dog, but when it showed its true form, it was a grotesque monster.

She couldn't take her eyes away. It was all so crazy. It wasn't a hideous creature he was mutating into. When the transformation was complete, he had become the most gorgeous hunk of male flesh she'd ever seen. She rubbed her eyes and looked again. Was she going insane? *Okay... I'm dreaming. There is no way this is real.* She pinched herself. *Wake up, Izzy.*

Antique Trove, a best-selling stand-alone story available at eXtasy Books and all online retailers.

EXCERPT:

It felt like hours had passed when the pounding of her heart finally simmered to a steady beat. She dared to open her eyes again and screamed. Directly in front of her stood an enormous reptile with wings. With a snap of its jaws, it lowered its head and glared at her. *What the hell? Is that a dragon? This is not happening.*

Dazed, she began to climb out of the chest. If she stepped clear, she would be back in her grandmother's shop, right?

"This is a dream. It is not real," Azilia muttered.

"This is no dream," the dragon said.

She must have lost her damn mind. Even though she was out of the chest, the hallucination was still there. She held her hands, palms out, in front of her body and took a careful step back. The last thing she wanted was to be this creature's lunch. "Okay. Now I know for sure I am dreaming or going crazy. Talking dragons?"

"You have finally come home," the dragon spoke again.

"Home?" *Oh, my God. I am actually answering the beast.*

She calmed down a bit. The dragon did not seem as if he wanted to gobble her up. It was actually quite beautiful with its shiny blue, purple, and red scales. But in all honesty? A talking dragon? And where in the gods' names was she? *This is just another one of my stupid nightmares.*

"No nightmare. I assure you I am very real."

Her eyes widened, and her jaw went slack. *Seriously? The damn creature is answering what I am thinking?* She felt kind of silly as she made a V with two fingers. "Peace..." Her voice came out like a squeaky little mouse.

An upcoming series:

Eye of the Gods 1

DARING CHAR

ABOUT THE AUTHORS

Taryn Jameson

Taryn Jameson is a mother, artist, and avid reader who lives in an enchanted forest that sparks her imagination to create. Her latest outlet is the written word. She is the alter ego of cover artist Angela Waters.

Gabriella Bradley

Gabriella Bradley has been a writer and artist all her life. Her hobbies include art, gardening, swimming, sewing, embroidery. Favorite movies are old timers like Gone with the Wind, Spartacus, etc. Favorite music is Abba. All-time favorite series is Fringe.